About the Author

Born in Bangladesh, Shukdeb Sen moved to Calcutta (now Kolkata), in India, he emigrated to the USA, and has spent a thirty-year career in teaching, research, and mentoring undergraduate students at various colleges and universities in the South. *Flower Still Blooms* is his first fiction book. *Black Education in White America* was his first non-fiction book. He has published over thirty research articles in scientific journals. He lives in Florida USA.

Flower Still Blooms

Shukdeb Sen

Flower Still Blooms

Olympia Publishers
London

www.olympiapublishers.com
OLYMPIA PAPERBACK EDITION

A CIP catalogue record for this title is
available from the British Library.

ISBN: 978-1-78830-795-6

This is a work of fiction.
Names, characters, places and incidents originate from the writer's
imagination. Any resemblance to actual persons, living or dead, is
purely coincidental.

First Published in 2020

Olympia Publishers
Tallis House
2 Tallis Street
London
EC4Y 0AB

Printed in Great Britain

Dedication

In memory of Bhudeb Sen my brother, and my wife
Sulakshana for her patience and support.
With love and gratitude.

PREFACE

Flower Still Blooms is a collection of short stories written over fifteen years and the book describes the human experiences reflected on behavior; it is a paradox, ranging from altruism and compassion on one side to torturous injustice, predator driven carnal passion that subsumes everything through death!

An age-old human quest for the meaning of life is why me? Why do I suffer? Does God exist? Or is Godhead an imagination created by humans as a scaffolding of protection from a consuming fear of the vastness of the universe, and insignificant existence?

All these questions are the essence of humanity.

Many stories in this collection project a sense of deep pessimism, and hopelessness, but elevate human innate desire to live based on resilience, and belief yet to appear in the horizon which is rested or anchored in hope.

The flower still blooms!

FLOWER STILL BLOOMS

It was a nice mild autumn day in Calcutta. I stood in the middle of the entrance to the great white Victoria Memorial Hall courting everybody to enter the building. I have stood here for many decades, as a matter of fact; many people admired me more than the real white building. Many people remarked that this memorial for Queen Victoria is a disgrace to the Indian culture and heritage. The British forced the people to build this memorial, so they could remember their Queen as the Taj Mahal. But it was a failure. They tried to copy Taj, but that was an impossible task. So it was a white building built on nothing but emptiness. My job was to stand guard near that lifeless white marble monument. I had been carrying those chores for ages, not happily, but what else could I do? After all, I was a horse — a statue made of bronze.

I had seen a lot through my eyes. I remembered the day when the Prince of Wales opened the gate in 1921. It was a grand occasion. The British Empire was on top of the world and the Queen of England had everything in her hand. Pageantry, pompous English nobility, and sahibs gave a good show. It thrilled me and I was proud to be there.

As time passed, the light of England dimmed. The Bengali people revolted against the British oppression and tyranny. Then the revolution came, and the revolutionary leaders like Surya Sen, Subhash Chandra Bose, Aurobindo, Khudiram, and others. The lolling fires of revolution in Bengal shook the foundation of the great British Empire. I have seen and heard many courageous acts of the people and their supreme sacrifice for their freedom.

At last the freedom came. India was free from colonialism, but it divided the country. Many millions became homeless; millions died because of religious carnage. The whole place was in shambles. I cried in despair. I could not believe that life meant nothing to other human beings. It was a strange feeling. The sculptor who made me from a blob of bronze was a kind man. He had respect and love for everything. With tenderness he gave me my shape, my life and everything. But how could the same human race be so ruthless? I sometimes cannot understand; maybe a horse is more humane than the real human.

Whenever I go back to the past, I become emotional and paranoid; let me look on the bright side of the life — the present. Yes, it was a nice autumn day. The breeze was pleasant; it rubbed my back with a gentle sweep. I was happy. They cleaned my face, no pockmarks inscribed on me yet by the ruthless wet acidic rain. I was handsome and graceful. Many commented about my beautiful eyes; I felt shy at the same time I was thankful to those peoples who were my admirers.

The noise of tram cars, lorries, buses, the rickshaws, and human voices had died down as dark approached over the whole city. The sky was grayish and getting ready to welcome the full moon. The phosphorescent lights blinked for a few seconds and then stared all over us with a bright smile. My friend the great Saal tree stood there erect in defiance of gravity and its generous crown of leaves embraced the breeze.

The shade provided shelter to people in rain; it was a cool resting place during the summer, and a sanctuary for lovers under its shadow in the spring. This shelter was always available and ready for occupation.

This evening I could see a young woman standing under the Saal tree. She was a newcomer; I have never seen her before. She was young and pretty. She was wearing a sari made up of nylon and her pretty face was filled with melancholy. Her sadness created a lattice of light and shade in the air. I was curious about her.

The breeze suddenly became a little gusty. It caressed the fleshy corners of the young woman with a fury, as if it had never seen young flesh, nor touched it before. This thin transparent sari was trying to fly away with the gust, but the young woman wrapped her sari tightly over her body, as if she needed protection from someone.

A man with a stare of a Jackal was looking at her from a short distance. He was smoking a cigarette with great pleasure. The cigarette glowed in darkness as a bellow attached to the up and down motion of the ribcage. The man sucked the white smoke of tobacco inside his mouth and released it through controlled spasms of puckered lips making circles. Gusty wind picked up the white circles of smoke and smeared them over the young woman's body with lust. The wind and the jackal-eyed man were enjoying the whole episode. I felt like screaming for this rape — the inhuman torture of this young woman. But I was mute-sound, movement and other infallible rights of a living creature were not given to me. I was a statue!

The young woman broke the silence and with a tearful voice said, "Was it too much to ask for Rs.20? Do you know we have eaten nothing for two days? My little brother is waiting for me at our home inside the concrete water pipe."

The jackal-eyed man came close by, grabbed her hand and placed a five-rupee banknote on her palm. He walked away from her and uttered in disgust, "Hell, whatever I got playing cards, that little dough slipped away from my hand."

He tossed the cigarette butt on the grass, squashed it with rage by his shoes and spat at it with infinite hate.

As the wind renewed its attack with the gust, it noticed that the woman was crying. The five-rupee note was soaked in tears. The freedom to cry was there. There were no more obstacles; no more inhibitions to express the melancholy of life. Hungry, thirsty dry soil drank every bit of those warm tears and thanked for this gift.

The wind subsided as if it showered its warm body with a cool, salty tears and it felt ashamed of its behavior. The squashed cigarette released its last breath through a veil of white smoke; it danced like a snake and dissipated in oblivion.

Blooming Rajani Gandha spread their sweet fragrance all over the place and declared in silence that the flower still blooms in this earth.

A VULTURE AND A CHILD

The court of the God

In the center of the cosmos, God lives in his kingdom. A vulture, a malnourished, starving child, and Yama (the death), came to the court to get judgment from the God, whether the boy must die or should he continue to live.

The vulture asked permission from God to speak first, why must the boy die?

God replied, "You can give reasons why the boy must die."

The vulture said, "I need food to survive. I have starved for a long time and I must eat; otherwise I might succumb to death because of starvation. I am not yet ready to die."

God asked the vulture, "Just because you are starved, you want this child to die, so you can live?"

The vulture replied, "Yes, my existence depends on his death. If he lives, then I will die through starvation, and that will end my existence." The vulture continued, "Almighty God, please understand, the existence of 'I' is the essence of living. If I do not exist, then nothing exists".

God smiled at the vulture and said, "So you want to exist, but you do not care about the child who also exists and wants to exist. Your existence is very important to you but the child's existence is responsible for your impending non-existence so you want the child to die so you can live."

The vulture realized that he was a selfish and self-centered being. He felt dejected and sad that he was a mean and an uncaring vulture.

The God asked the child, "Why do you want to die so young?"

The child replied, "I want to die so I can be free. Death is the only way for me to live in freedom. The life I am experiencing is filled with starvation, disease, and neglect and is not the life I wanted to live. I came here as an accident. I did not choose to be here. My existence is filled with sadness, hopelessness, and nothingness, but still I exist. This battered body filled with diseases and filth, still carries my existence, which can satisfy the hunger of the vulture and can nourish him and provide strength so he can exist. If I die, then the vulture will eat my body and restore his health. I will attain my freedom and I will be free."

It surprised the God to hear the child's desire to sacrifice his life so that the vulture could live. By dying the child would be free. The child did not want to be born, but it happened not by divine interference, but in a moment of physical lust that created this human birth. Life is an accident!

God then looked at Yama, and asked, "Yama, whom would you take with you in the palace of death, where nothingness consumes the existence?"

Yama for the first time in his existence did not know the answer. He replied, "Oh Omnipotent Almighty, why are you tormenting my soulless existence? You know well that if the time is right then only I can execute my power of death that I am carrying."

God replied with a somber voice, "Yama, you have failed the test. The time is not infinite, it is finite, and you are the

16

chosen one to guard and regulate it."

The vulture flapped its wings and asked, "If the time is not right, then death cannot touch the existence; hence we all must live so that our existence can exist."

God nodded at vulture's explanation and said to Yama, "You must extend the time for the vulture and the child, so they can live for a long time."

Yama touched the vulture with his shining spear and made the vulture a well-nourished, healthy, much younger looking vulture. Then God nodded and said, "Well done Yama". Then Yama looked at the child and pointed his spear to touch the child but the child extracted all his energy from his feeble body to generate a thunderous command, "Stop! You may not take away my freedom. You must take me to your palace of death where I belong, because you have the power to bring infinite time to a finite existence and give me the privilege of being free through death."

It perplexed Yama, and he could not move his spear. He was angry and felt insulted and impotent to act. His body transformed into a monster whose glowing red eyes burning like a hearth to incinerate the child like a flash. The child did not flinch. Fear of burning alive did not deter his desire to be free.

It shocked the God to see Yama's attitude and it said to Yama, "Shame on you. You have lost your temper and are trying to bully a little child to obey your unfair wishes."

Yama felt God's rebuke. He came back to his senses and apologized to God and the child.

The child begged the God to convince Yama to take him to the palace of death where he could achieve his freedom.

The child's selfless desire to die moved God so he could achieve his freedom. God summoned the keeper of time.

The keeper of time, a silhouette of a hunchback, appeared in the court in a flash. God looked at the timekeeper, and asked, "What should you do to satisfy the desire of the child to be free?"

The time keeper looked at the child, the vulture, Yama, and the God, then said, "Let the child live with health and prosper in life so that his existence can be forever embedded into his smile. As long as the smile of the child and innocence lives in him/her, then he/she is free."

The timekeeper's action/solution pleased God and he said, "Job well done".

Yama was not happy to hear the solution given by the timekeeper. He said, "This idea will allow all children to be free from death and live forever. This will change the balance of life and death."

The boy smiled and said, "Now I am free."

Vulture was very pleased as well. Only Yama, the carrier of death was not pleased at all. He whimpered with frustration and disbelief as he asked God, "Why did you accept the timekeeper's solution and left me wondering how I fit in this scheme of things? Why did you keep me in the palace of death to erase existence from everyone? Just take me away from this job and leave me some place in this universe where I can exist not as a creature who exists for the sake of existence!"

God raised his hand and ordered Yama to be free from death. He proclaimed that he also existed and was not a figment of the imagination of human creation, as humans liked to think. Existence is a reality as the universe exists for the sake of existence!

THE TRAIN

It was Saturday, May 5, 1979. I was waiting for the train to Paris at Midi station in Bruxelles. A bearded man approached me and said, "How far would you be going?"

"Paris, Gare du Nord," I said.

"Oh, how nice, I am going there too. Would you mind if I sit and talk with you for a while?"

I didn't like his direct intrusion into my journey, but I had nothing else to do, so I thought to have someone to talk to during the three-hour train ride would be pleasant enough.

"It will a pleasure for me to talk with you," I said.

He sat by me on a bench in the railway station. He was very curious about me and asked many questions about my profession and me. I didn't like his directness either but got along well with him; I had nothing to hide. He was in his early sixties, spoke fluent English and had a Star of David around his neck. He was thrilled to know that I was a writer. He asked me if he could interest me in his story.

Naturally, I was interested, so I said to him, "I will be happy to hear your story."

The express train for Paris arrived in the station on time. We hopped into the first-class compartment and sat face to face close to the window. I was studying him. He was well built with piercing eyes and a long nose. He opened his small travel bag, took out an apple, peeled the skin with one incision and disposed of the long coil of reddish apple skin in the wastebasket and offered me a piece which I accepted. After a few moments of silence, he straightened his arched back and started his story…

"It was spring of 1943 and I was only twenty-five then. Hitler had just rounded up all the Jews from Belgium and shipped them to France. We landed up in Chateauneuf-les-Bains Camp. From there they shipped us like cattle in the stockyard trains to the death camp of Dachau; it was one of the worst train journeys, a human being could take. In any case we arrived in Camp C where the Commandant was cruel and savage. His name was Hermann Hoss. I was fortunate to have a job as the gardener for the Commandant. Monique Beaujolin, a French communist, was the maid in the Commandant's house. We faced hard back-breaking forced labor, beatings by Capo and the Gestapo. The Capo and SS men raped women regularly.

"Many of us gave in to this inhuman existence. Some committed suicide; others tried to get favors from the guards by enslaving themselves. I was lucky to get the job as a gardener. Even to this day I am not sure how and why I was chosen as a gardener.

"Every day new batches of prisoners arrived in the camp, and in the night, many headed for the crematorium or a long journey to the Polish border and then to Auschwitz. It was like an eternal cycle. Our living conditions were so bad we could not even stretch our bodies during the night. Many died because of exhaustion, malnutrition, dysentery, typhus and torture.

"Monique was a bright young girl. She knew that her life was short, and she would die soon. As a communist her chance to live was short. She wanted to be free. To gain her freedom from physical torture, she became a total slave to Commandant Hoss, and he used her for his carnal obsession.

"Besides taking care of the Commandant's garden, I used to deliver fresh flowers to his house. One morning I cut fresh roses and took them to the house. Monique, the maid usually would open the door and take the flowers inside. But that day the Commandant's wife opened the door. I handed her the flowers and said, "Good morning, madam."

"She smiled at me and asked me to come inside. I was scared and hesitated for a while. But she signaled with her finger for me to come in. I entered the living room. 'Put those flowers on the table,' she ordered.

"I placed the flowers in the vase. My hands were trembling with an unknown fear. Death loomed always over our shoulders. The prisoners of the concentration camp knew that their time was short. They were dead. Even though their hearts still pumped, they could walk and think but they were living corpse. 'Look at me,' she commanded with a low voice. I looked at her. She was wearing a red velvet robe. She unfastened her robe; her milky white breasts exposed themselves. She was not wearing any underclothing, only the robe. My whole body started to tremble; my blood froze; whole body was dead cold. I couldn't move, my heartbeat slowed down, I was in a quasi-death condition. I could not think; my mind was blank. My mouth was bitter and dry; no traces of moisture inside, only tears came to my eyes. She came close, wiped the tears from my eyes and said, 'Don't be scared, I will be your friend if you would give me what I want.'"

"I was mute; only tears flowed from my eyes. 'Don't you

21

want freedom? I know why you are so frightened! Don't be afraid of me. I am a prisoner as you are. I want my freedom too. You could provide me that,' she said.

"I couldn't understand what was happening; it totally lost me. She asked me to sit down and touch her body. I didn't want to touch her, because I knew that would be like committing suicide. Her husband would put a bullet in my head, and I would be dead within seconds. I was not yet ready to die. The gas chamber was waiting for me, but still I had time to live.

"'Touch me, caress me, and kiss me now. You must obey me; otherwise I will make sure you die,' she uttered in a whisper. This death sentence whipped me in the pit of my stomach, and someone charged me with sexual passion. I thought if I didn't obey her orders I would die, and if I obeyed her orders, then I might have a chance of survival. There was no point of thinking about death because I was a living death, so I might as well fulfill my libido for the last time before my physical death. That thought gave me strength, and I got up, caressed her body, and with tremendous passion, fulfilled our sexual desire.

"I left the house counting the minutes before the summons for death would come. I was ready to die because a dying person shouldn't be afraid of death. Death would be my freedom...

"Time passed. The death summons did not come. Instead, I received a note from Franca, the Commandant's wife. It said, 'Bring some roses tomorrow morning.'

"The next morning, I took red roses from the garden and arrived in front of the Commandant's house. I pressed the doorbell. Monique didn't answer but Franca did. I entered the room. She wore the same velvet robe. She hugged me, and we merged our bodies like two lovers who were in love. That day Franca told me her story. Commandant Hoss was an impotent man; his sexual inadequacy camouflaged under tyranny, torture and murderous lust. He loved to abuse women. Monique knew how to handle him, because she gave her flesh to him for his total pleasure and she fulfilled all of his carnal fantasies so she could get favors from him.

"Her husband never satisfied Franca. He never cared about her or her needs. He was selfish and cruel with her, used to beat her whenever he felt like. She contemplated suicide many times but her fear of mutilation of her beautiful body prevented her from doing so. She decided to have an affair, knowing that if someone exposed this affair, then both of us would die. She reached a point where she preferred death rather than this intolerable life in a death camp.

"Our affair lasted for about three months. We used to get together whenever Commandant Hoss went out. I suspected that Monique knew about the whole thing, and it worried me that she might disclose our relationship to the Commandant. One day I asked Franca what she would do if Herman Hoss found out about our affair. She replied, 'I would tell him it is better to live a short life with satisfaction and love, than a long life with frustration, despised and with unfulfilled desire. This unfulfilled life is not a living entity but death.'

"Everybody wants their freedom. Freedom has many shades, so much color and verve, at the same time it is paradoxical. By dying you gain your freedom, but is it really freedom? Being alive you are free to exist, but it curtails your freedom of expression and existence; it dehumanizes you. You are a living dead, without your freedom," I said.

"'By dying if you could gain your freedom from torture,

sufferings, dehumanization, and indifference then that death is freedom. Your existence must exist within this cosmos only when you are living to enjoy the beauty, love, and happiness of this life. But if that existence is denied, then your existence no longer exists. You are a void. Physical entity is not the existence, but the true, fulfilling being is the existence — it is the freedom,' she answered.

"We gazed at each other for some time in silence. Then I asked her if we could escape from this concentration camp. She looked at me and said, 'We cannot escape together, but if you want your freedom, then I could arrange that. Maybe someday I will see you again.' Tears came to my eyes. Even within this Hell, humanity existed.

"Franca arranged a pass for me to go into town to get supplies for her embroidery. One young German guard took me to the town, which was about one hundred kilometers from the camp. The Swiss border was far from the town, but I had to take a chance. That was an opportunity for me to be free. The jeep was running along the hilly countryside. I had to decide at what point I should try to kill this German soldier so I could be free. My companion was young just like me. He was full of life, but I was determined to eliminate him from my life so I could be alive. On our way back from the town I decided that the time was right for me to act. The young soldier was happily whistling a German tune, and suddenly, I grabbed the steering wheel and swerved the steering wheel forcefully on the left, which surprised him. He was trying to keep the car on its proper course and he cursed me. At that moment of confusion, I pulled his gun out from the holster and shot him in the chest. The car was out of control, and I jumped out. The car crashed on the rocky walls of the hill and then fell into a ditch where it ignited into flames. I ran through the meadows as fast as I could. The faster I moved through the hills toward the Swiss border, I would have a better chance of freedom."

Mr. Isaac Rosenthal paused for a moment and then said, "Well, I escaped. I was free." He became silent. I was very curious about the fate of the others. But he didn't utter a word. Only silence crept through the railway compartment. I was restless and couldn't tolerate that cold silence from him. The fate of other persons was puzzling me. I couldn't bear that silence, hence, I asked, "What happened to Franca? What happened to Monique? Did they survive?" He looked at me with a blank gaze in his eyes, and then he muttered, "Yes, both of them got their freedom."

I was very happy to know that, so I said, "Well, at least three of you escaped from death." He looked at me; tears dripped from his eyes and said, "They got their freedom by dying".

A cold silence fell between us. I realized that Mr. Rosenthal was no longer in this train; his mind flew back to the concentration camp where their short-lived love bloomed into life… but the question still hovered over me. How did Monique die? I could see how Franca died, but Monique? I had to know the whole story; otherwise my mind would be restless.

"So". I asked, "Mr. Rosenthal, please tell me how Monique died?" Mr. Rosenthal looked at me and said, "Monique wanted her freedom so she disclosed everything to Herman Hoss in the belief he would give her freedom. He shot Franca the next day for having an affair with a Jew and let Monique go free for her loyalty towards him. Monique was free in the meadows of the hell, but they cut her freedom short by a bullet from a German sharpshooter. He kept his promise to Monique to give her freedom. All this I came to know — at the end of the war — from Alice, a close friend of Monique."

The train was running close to seventy-five miles an hour. He was free. The shrill of the train whistle reminded us that life was real. Mr. Rosenthal was silent. He was communicating with the spirit of Franca, Monique and thousands of other human beings who died with no reason.

The train arrived on time at the Gare du Nord. I shook Mr. Rosenthal's hand and said, "Goodbye. Thank you very much for the story." He bowed his head in silence and walked away with the crowd.

THE LITTLE MERMAID

It was drizzling outside. I could see through my hotel window how the wind swirled drizzle into a turbulent burst of hard rain where raindrops metamorphosed into big bubbles of air splattered on the window pane. I thought I'd go out to the harbor and walk in the garden to enjoy the softness of a cool morning. But a strong wind with heavy rain dampened my desire to go out. I laid on my bed and relaxed. A few minutes passed by, and I felt in my hair a soft blow of air that brought a cool sensation to my body. That sensation aroused a desire — a strange mental urge to get up and see the little mermaid sitting atop large boulders in the harbor.

I got up from my bed and dressed up with rain proof-jacket and boots to tackle the rain and marched toward the harbor where the world-famous little mermaid sat in a melancholic posture waiting for the man she loved. My hotel was only a few blocks away. Most of the time this area was filled with tourists from around the world, wanting to see the beautiful little mermaid sculpted by a great sculptor Edvard Eriksen. This morning the rain prevented people, except a few like me, who were attracted to the statue like an obsession.

The wind picked up and carried rain in a blinding rage. The waves swelled up and crashed on the boulders with a vengeance. The strong gargling sound of the crashing waves topped with foams danced around the boulders where the little mermaid sat. I went close to the ramp where steps were made over the boulders, so that people could see the statue up close. Swelling seas submerged a few steps of the rampart. I sat on the highest step of the ramp and looked down at the melancholic face of the little mermaid. Rain subsumed the face, bosom, groin, and fins of the mermaid as if a monster trying to strangle her. I sat there motionless, looking at the mermaid. The rain pelted relentlessly at my eyes and created a misty film which took away complete transparency of my vision.

I was glued to her beautiful melancholic, serene, and expectation filled gaze. My misty eyes noticed a slight movement in her gaze. It was a soft gesture that shifted in rain-filled bubbles. That gesture was trying to tell me something. It mesmerized me, I stood up and went down to the steps of the ramp. Rushing waves splashed on the rocks that touched my feet, as I moved forward close to the large boulders. I felt cold water engulf my body above my waist. I could see little mermaid much more clearly even with the heavy rain forming a water canopy over her body.

Suddenly, I felt someone grab me from behind and pull me with a great force, stopping my forward movement. I fell in a murky, turbulent pool of water, and a man held my hands to pull me away from the rushing water current. I gulped a lot of salty water and came to my senses. I was almost heading for deep water without knowing where I was going. A very tall man wearing a local fisherman's yellow raincoat pulled me away from the swirling water and saved me from drowning.

A small crowd including Danish security personnel gathered around me. A tall man with a cap asked me with a deep accent why I was approaching the statue so closely in a rainstorm. What was my motive? What was my nationality and many other questions in rapid succession?

I ingested a large amount of water and my mind was not yet cognitively tuned in to the circumstances I was in. My speech was disturbed but I tell the gentleman I went close to the statue to see her. I intentionally hid the fact that I felt the mermaid signaled to me to come close to her. That answer would have confirmed that I was a mentally sick person, and capable of committing suicide or other things like that.

The tall man with the cap asked me, "Just to see her closely, you went in the rushing water in the stormy weather?"

I replied, "Yes, that was my intent."

He asked me where I was from and what my nationality was.

I said, "I'm an American citizen and live in the States."

By this time my mind recuperated from this unusual out-of-body experience. I realized that this gentleman was a Danish police officer, and he was questioning my motive, if I were a member of some political group who deliberately wanted to disfigure, deface or damage the statue to vent their political beliefs or other activities against the Danish government's action toward the Iraq war or killing whales?

I explained to him I was a tourist from the USA and I had no intention of harming the statue which I adored very much.

The tall man frisked me to see if I had any objects I might use to deface the bronze statue. He found nothing except my cellphone. He tried to click my phone to see if it worked or not. The cellphone lit up even though it was soaked in water. He asked me to punch my password to see if there was any hidden explosive programmed with it to blow up the statue. The cellphone opened and waited for further instruction from me. The man chuckled, and said, "It is working fine."

I said, "It is a great and reliable phone."

He said, "Enjoy your stay in Copenhagen," and left.

The rain had subsided by now. More people gathered around the statue. I looked at the statue and noticed that melancholic face with expectation of her mate's arrival was shrouded in liquid drops of rain as if the tears of her eyes were flowing like a stream where unfulfilled love waited in eternity!

I was wondering about the gesture I experienced in the little mermaid's rain-soaked face. Was it real, or an illusion in my mind's eye that subsumed my own cognitive existence? Was it a feeling metamorphosed into a solidarity on the mermaid's loneliness and expectation that is inscribed in the depth of finite time? Or was it my feeling of loneliness, agony and void of my life's existence hijacked my visual perception into a neuronal impulse that reflect attributes of motion? Was it an apparition from the Eriksen's creation that fooled men's desire to be with her, where time and space were frozen for infinity?

Answers of all these possibilities may not be found and/or rationalized, but one thing is for sure I will cherish this out-of-body experience forever as long as I live.

HOPE

It was a mild June day in Lausanne, Switzerland. I was waiting for the train to go to Schilthorn. The summer was approaching. In the railway station waiting room, I noticed two young ladies in their mid-twenties were sitting in the waiting area's corner room. The two young ladies were close. They were holding their hands, their smiling faces adoring each other's presence with absolute tenderness. Their eyes were radiating with a glow that signified that they were in love. I was imbibing in their tenderness like a thirsty pheasant who had not drank for a long time. I was curious about them, trying to figure out if they were French, German, Swiss, Italian, or British. They were speaking English with a deep accent, not British or Irish, perhaps some countries from the African continent. My curious, roving eyes attracted their attention. I tried to hide my curious eyes away from theirs, but to no avail. One girl pointed at me, and said to the other girl, "Look at that man who is eating us alive with his piercing eyes, I guess he must be from India. What you think Monica?"

"I think you are right. Please don't speak so loudly. He could hear you Barbara."

"I don't care. I want him to hear me. He is eating me alive with his eyes."

Then both the girls burst into laughter. I was embarrassed and felt like a thief getting caught in a bad deed in front of everybody. Fortunately, at that moment the railway intercom announced that the train for Schilthorn would arrive at track number three in three minutes. I got out from the waiting room and rushed towards the track number three. The Swiss people and their machines were always on time. This country ran like a clock, never missing a beat as if life depended on time.

I sat by the window seat in a first-class coach. I bought an Eurorail pass so I could travel around Europe. Those two young ladies entered the same coach and sat opposite me, facing me. I tossed an embarrassed, shy smile at them and they reciprocated. One girl introduced herself as Monica and asked, "How far would you go?"

"Schilthorn," I replied.

"What a coincidence! We are going to Schilthorn as well."

"Wonderful! My journey will be a memorable one because of you two pretty ladies," I replied with enthusiasm.

Both the girls blushed... The train was in full speed.

Both Monica and Barbara were secretaries, working for some import-export company in Salisbury. They had met each other on a tennis court and became close friends. Monica had blue eyes with freckles all over her face and the well-developed cleavage I could see through her nylon blouse. She had curly, brownish hair flowing over her shoulder. Occasionally, she twisted her shoulder length hair with a delicate, well-manicured hand. Her fingernails were painted with a glossy pink shade. She had a smile which dispatched a passionate desire. Barbara showed a rugged profile, filled with small pimple scars on her face. She had brown eyes with a piercing brightness that gave an impression that her life was tough and harsh. Two opposite characters but in unison they appeared to be very happy, united and in love.

The train zoomed through the mountainous broad-gauge railway track like a serpent; it passed by the most beautiful wine producing area of Switzerland. After Fribourg we arrived at Bern, the capital of Switzerland. We had to change the train and headed towards Interlaken. At Interlaken we boarded another train with the narrow-gauge railway to Lauterbrunnen. Once we arrived in Lauterbrunnen, we had to catch the postal bus coach to reach Stechelberg. The postal bus snaked along the narrow mountainous road slowly. I noticed on our right-hand side the magnificent Murrenbach Falls gushing over the cliff with a thundering noise. The thunderous falls created a mist where reflecting sun beams danced in rainbows. Monica came to my side to see this beautiful waterfall, and at that moment her cheek brushed my cheek which created a sensuous pleasure throughout my whole body.

From Stechelberg we took the cableway. The enchanting mountain hamlet surrounded by alpine meadows, cool breezes and close body contact between us, made me feel romantic. The cable car rose almost vertically to over five thousand feet. We stopped at Murren, then changed to another cable car which was smaller than the previous one. The empty space between us was almost gone; we were pressed to each other. I could feel the deep breath of Monica and Barbara; they pressed their bosoms against my chest...

We arrived in Schilthorn via Brig with a steep ascent to a height of almost ten thousand feet. We got out of the cableway and saw the Piz Gloria, the revolving restaurant on the mountain's top. In front of us the majestic Alps wearing its white coat of snow. It was freezing; as far as your eyes could see only snow — a mass of frigid existence. A few black birds were spotted here and there in the snow. One could see Swiss lowland on one side, on the other side is the Alpine range crowned by the gigantic Eiger, Monch and Jungfrau. It was a magical place. In that peaceful, solemn place you forgot the trials and tribulations of the daily life; your mind and soul filled with a joy which had not yet experienced before.

Three of us sat at a table in the restaurant, ordered sandwiches and wine, ate our food slowly enjoying this beautiful place and each other's company. After our lunch we moved to the sun terrace, made a snowman with powdery snow and played for a while throwing snowballs at each other. When we were almost frozen, we huddled together to soak up the remaining warmth radiating from our bodies. We were like three young souls marooned on top of the Alps.

On our way back, we stopped at Murren, walked around the scenic village and took the funicular to arrive at Lauterbrunnen. The brightness of the sunshine defused as evening approached slowly like a melancholy engulfing the happiness. It was 5:30. We had to wait an hour and a half before our train to Interlaken would arrive in Lauterbrunnen. Monica suggested eating snacks in a cafe close by. We sat outside on a table and ordered fondue made up with different local cheeses including Gruyere. The locals served fondue in a bowl kept hot by small burning candle underneath. It was customary to dip a piece of bread into the molten cheese, enjoying the delicate flavor of this famous Swiss culinary delight. All three of us shared our meal from the same bowl of cheese as our race, country of origin all melted into a homogenous mixture of humanity.

The train for Interlaken arrived in the station exactly at 7:00 just like clockwork. We entered the first-class coach and sat next to the window seats. I could see a sad gloom covering Barbara's rough face; I was clueless what was happening to her and kept silent. Monica asked me, "Shukumar do you believe in God?"

"Well, I have an idea about God, but I am not sure whether or not I believe in Him. Eastern philosophy of a supreme being gave the western civilization a light of hope and faith on which it could flourish. The lofty idealism of Christianity grew out of eastern mysticism. They transformed the image of God into the life of Jesus Christ against the injustices and sufferings. Why do you ask this question Monica?" I said.

"Next month our country Rhodesia will change into a new country called Zimbabwe. I am afraid of the day when this ultimate change will occur. That day our fate will also change. I can see that Barbara and I will be stranded in the city: no jobs, no prospect of a meaningful living in a hostile city. The life itself will be a question mark. I cannot even think what is waiting for us in Zimbabwe. The sheer thought brings an uncontrollable shiver of death."

"Why are you so pessimistic about life? Life is real. It has good and bad sides, and otherwise there will be no existence. Your fear of being totally destitute is groundless. Give a chance so that humanity can survive the struggle. The blacks and all other colored people have been oppressed, tortured, and dehumanized but still they have survived. They have always asked the Almighty that they could get their freedom. The shackle of ignorance, injustice and slavery be lifted from their body, mind, and soul, so they could live like human beings. The time has dawned in Rhodesia when people of all races and creeds can see themselves as humans," I said.

"White settlers colonized Rhodesia in the late nineteenth

35

century. Many whites with the support of the Rhodesian government have tortured and killed thousands of black people over the years. They have subjugated them, dehumanized them but we have done no harm to anybody. I have always felt that black majority should rule the country. But now I feel I have to pay the price for the others who have tormented and enslaved the black people in Rhodesia. I am innocent, but my innocence will not protect me from being mistreated or abused," Monica muttered.

"It is unfortunate and unjustified but for someone's injustice, intolerance, oppression, and murderous action would inflict mortal damage to innocent people who have done no harm to anybody. Those innocent people become the victims and they have to pay with their life to justice. The nature is ruthless. The fire destroys everything living close to it, but at the end, it clears the path through the ashes to spring forward a new generation filled with hope and prosperity for all," I said.

"God is almighty and omnipotent. He will protect us from injustice. I pray all the time and I believe in Him. He will sustain us," Barbara said.

"I don't think that will happen. If God was there, then how come He allowed those colored people to go through inhuman sufferings? He did not care about them. Their agonized, tormented soul asked for His mercy and help, but God ignored their call; injustice and torture prevailed. He is not there. The human animals have killed Him long, long ago. He is dead! Ask nothing from Him, because he is a void, non-existing entity," I said.

"It cannot be. He is there. His mercy will fall up on us," Monica whispered.

A smile played on my lips that brought a sharp look from Barbara in disbelief and she asked me, "Are you an atheist?"

"I am not an atheist, but I am searching for that elusive, omnipotent, omnipresent, Godhead who could provide me some answer about the sufferings of human race in this world. The more I see, analyze, and deduce from facts, I conclude that God is absent. Some opportunists who wanted to gain power through His existence created Him."

Barbara held my hand in her palms. Her eyes melted into tears and with a trembling voice filled with unknown fear, she asked, "Do you think we survive this sudden change?"

"Yes, you will survive this drastic change in your country. Give a chance to the oppressed people. Have faith and trust in them. If we do not have faith in humanity, then we have nothing as a human race. We all will die. First, we must have faith within ourselves. We must have the desire to live in harmony so we can live. People are afraid of the unknown; we have created a vacuum in anticipation of the unknown, but we humans must muster the courage to face the unknown then we can conquer our fear. We will emancipate ourselves from despair filled with fear and it would resurrect us. The life is beautiful; darkness is always there but a shining light pierces through the darkness of life. Come out of the shadow of doubts, have courage and faith in humanity."

Both of them embraced me. Tears flowing from our eyes glistened by the fluorescent light of the cabin, giving a ray of hope for the future of the human race.

MELON KING

It was a summer night. The full moon was shining brightly in the sky. Moonlight danced on the tiny waves created by the blowing warm wind caressing the surface of the lake. Floating patches of clouds played hide and seek with the moonlight. Scattered log cabins and their inhabitants were deep in sleep.

Dawn approached the sleepy village, radiating its light on the horizon. The sound of a bugle cracked open the serenity of the place. The sleepy village woke up from its slumber as if a blow from the whip stroke its flesh!

Men, women, boys, and girls lined up on the field as the overseer called their name and recorded their presence. Then everybody dashed to the massive field to start their jobs — hoeing, planting, and cleaning the field. In the middle of the vast expanse field workers made a huge watermelon patch where large dark brown and deep green striped watermelons lay in neat rows. This was the home of King's great sweet watermelon field in Dooly County, Georgia.

Scott King was the owner of this plantation. His plantation produced cotton, corn, potatoes, timber, and watermelons. He was very proud to grow the sweetest watermelon in Georgia and proclaimed himself as the king of melon. He was a stocky fellow, with a slight limp when he walked because of injury. When he was twelve years old, he tried to ride a horse which was not yet broken for the ride; the horse kicked him on the left side of his foot and broke the shinbone. Since then he walked with a limp. He loved to eat a watermelon, and he could spit the seeds a few yards away through a gap between his two front teeth.

Scott practiced a strange ritual each summer. Before harvesting the ripened watermelon from the field each year in May he asked all girls aged thirteen through nineteen to stand in the field, and he checked each young girl to see if the melon was right to harvest. He awarded the largest and roundest chested girl the queen of the melon patch for that year. In the night Scott came to the slave cabin and took away the girl to his pleasure cottage next to his residence for his carnal pleasure.

The girl chosen as the watermelon Queen must serve the wishes of Melon King; he will rape this young innocent girl. This was the part of the ritual during the watermelon harvest time. If any girl got pregnant because of rape, the girl must undergo a brutal procedure to extract the living embryo from the womb or the baby would be suffocated during the birthing process by a midwife and be pronounced a stillborn. They would bury the dead child in the jungle far from the plantation without a marker. No trace of the child would remain as animals would dig the grave and eat the remains. This way Scott erased all evidence of his rapes and fornication.

Scott King married a woman named Henrietta who was from Alabama. She was twenty-two years old when one of her relatives from her father's side brought a marriage proposal from a planter in Georgia. The plantar was a successful businessman, owning a large plantation in Dooly County, Georgia growing cotton, corn, timber, and watermelon. Henrietta's father Rev. Joseph Henry accepted the proposal and agreed to give his daughter Henrietta to Scott King for marriage. She entered Scott King's plantation as a queen who charmed every person in the plantation and other neighboring plantations around the small town known as Vienna.

Henrietta had deep blue eyes with dark eyebrows and she had a smile that sparkled like shining stars and was infectious enough to induce smiles from individuals around her. She was like a delicate flower, filled with fragrance and beauty that purified someone's sullen mood into a burst of sunshine glittering in the raindrops causing a rainbow. Henrietta received an education from her aunty who was a schoolteacher. She was a devout Christian and believed in Christ and faith through salvation.

Henrietta was a sweet Southern Belle liked by all people around the plantation. She treated everybody with kindness regardless of their race. Scott was not happy with Henrietta because she never accepted Scott's pleasure trips to the slave quarters during the middle of the night. It petrified all girls, and Scott enjoyed this torturous pleasure and showed his perverted masculinity because he was the master of this plantation. Mothers and fathers of the slave girls suffered this torture and bore these inhuman sufferings with no protest. They were helpless people and God ignored their cries, and prayer because God Himself was incapable of stopping this torment.

Mothers of raped girls would come to Henrietta and tell her of the sordid, inhuman torture of their innocent child by Scott. Henrietta held the hand of the crying mother and shed tears with them. Sometimes, Henrietta would ask God why the Omnipotent, Omnipresent Almighty would not take her away from this hellhole and liberate her. Henrietta many times told her husband to stop these cruel sadistic affairs, but Scott in a drunken state would abuse her by beating and calling Henrietta a Negro lover.

About a year after her marriage to Scott, Henrietta gave birth to a baby boy after a prolonged labor but because of excessive loss of blood she passed away. Henrietta achieved freedom through death as if God heard her cries and granted her freedom!

Henrietta's death made the baby boy an orphan. She told Scott when she was pregnant that if the baby was a boy, then name him Angel, and if it was a girl then Angelica. Scott never liked the child and wished he was dead!

Martha raised Angel along with her own child, a one-year-old named Tom. Her plentiful milk nourished Angel and gave him the best gift of life; to live and be healthy. Without it, Angel would have died along with his mother. Martha was Henrietta's favorite cook. She was agile, very attentive to the details, and a very organized person. She took care of all the needs of the household. Henrietta liked Martha's child Tom who was only one year old. Angel grew up with black children as there were no white boys or girls to play with on the plantation.

Martha's husband Solomon was a gardener, and they all lived in a small cottage next to the plantation house where Henrietta and Scott King had their bungalow. Henrietta loved roses and her garden was full of roses. Each spring the garden metamorphosed into a bright colored field, filled with fragrance of honeysuckle, jasmine, and roses. Solomon maintained the garden for his queen mistress Henrietta.

A couple of months after Henrietta's death, Scott broke up Martha's family so he could use Martha as a cook and personal pleasure and kept her in his bungalow. He realized it would be easier to sell Solomon and the baby to a Negro-trader so that Solomon could never see Martha again. This way Scott would force Martha to obey and fulfil all his carnal pleasure with no resistance from Solomon.

Martha pleaded and begged with Scott not to separate her from Solomon and the baby boy Tom, but he whipped her for disobeying his decision and showed everyone he was the master in the plantation. His desire and rule, was the supreme order and must be obeyed. If anyone violated this rule, they would receive fifteen lashes on the bare skin which would etch their mark on the flesh as a reminder. Martha cried days and night for the injustice done to her family. She asked God why He was punishing her. God never answered to her plea. Perhaps He did not want to listen to her, and only the sound of her heart wrenching cries pierced the space and lost to infinity.

Scott found a slave trader who sold Solomon to a plantation in New Orleans, and the baby to a middle-aged couple from Savannah, Georgia, who wanted a baby boy in their household so they could raise the baby and later they could sell him at a higher price.

Martha became a concubine of Scott and he kept his nightly pleasure visit to the slave quarters. Scott hated slaves but during the night in the darkness the carnal pleasure did not distinguish the color of black and white. Only the pleasure of dominance because of the power of money and authority dictated its supremacy and rule.

Scott loved to hunt. He rode his favorite white horse and chased after wild deer and shot them with his gun. He gave deer meat to his driver and overseer. He bragged about his hunting skill and mounted the head of a large buck in his study, where he kept his gun in a gun rack. He acquired various types of guns and revolvers. Every Friday night Scott went to the town and played cards with his friends and got drunk with moonshine and hard liquor. When he was drunk everybody avoided him because he showed frustration and rage towards his slaves, and with no provocation or reason picked on a person and started a fight. After Henrietta's death, Martha was often a hitting target for Scott. He would hit her with a cane and cursed her. Martha tolerated his behavior because she knew that she has no power to stop him. She pitied him, and at the same time condoned his violent behavior. Angel observed his father's behavior and stayed away from him. He hated his father for beating Martha.

Five years after Henrietta's death, Scott remarried to a woman from Savannah whose father had a big plantation growing rice. Her name was Adele. She was a strong-willed woman and hated everybody who was not white.

Adele slowly but steadily controlled Scott's life. She moved Martha from the cottage to the log cabins where other slaves lived. Adele prohibited Martha from entering the owner's bungalow where she used to live and cook for the whole family. Adele did not like Angel living with Martha and she asked Scott to keep Angel in the main house so she could teach Angel how to read and write. She took a special interest in home schooling. Angel wanted to stay with other children in the log cabins and play with them. He moved to the bungalow but was very unhappy about this separation from other children and Martha.

Adele developed a jealousy against Martha because everybody loved Martha for her sweet disposition, charming behavior, and efficiency. By moving Angel away from Martha,

Adele fulfilled her desire to hurt Martha. Martha cried for days over losing Angel. She felt a strong resentment against God, as she blamed Him for taking Solomon, Tom, and Angel away from her. She asked God why He was punishing her and taking away everything — what little happiness she was trying to hold onto in her life? Why was God not sparing her from the sufferings? Maybe it'd be great if He took her away from this wretched life and gave her freedom to be dead where only the echo of death would dance around in an empty void!

Scott realized that his authority to control the plantation life was over, and Adele was the master, and he had to obey orders from Adele. A strict regimen of control from Adele led Scott to drinking and he often arrived home in the evening drunk. His behavior changed also, as he became more violent towards his slaves and people around him. However, he feared Adele and never dared to hit her.

Even though Adele hated all slaves, she earned a lot of respect from her slaves because she could control Scott's amorous adventure. All female slaves were safe from the clutches of Scott. He spared the girls and women from rape but he increased his sadistic violent behavior towards them. A little altercation in the field such as slowing down plucking weeds, sowing seeds, cutting grain with a sickle, or slight resting was punishable by five to ten lashes by the cowhide whips. Each lash left a deep bloody mark on the back.

Adele could not bear a child for Scott. She blamed Scott for his sexual philandering and alcohol abuse denied Adele from having a child of her own. This made Adele a frustrated woman and led to her hating Angel more. Adele knew Angel loved Martha deeply and he would call Martha his "mommy". Angel's love for Martha and Adele's childless existence caused a jealousy against Martha that compounded Adele's hatred towards Angel. Angel was not fond of his father and stepmother. But he appreciated Adele's effort to help him as an educated person.

Time flew by, Angel was now fifteen years old, and he learned how to use the gun to hunt for rabbits, turkey, and possum. He would go to the forest with John, the overseer of the plantation to hunt for small animals just for fun. He became a good hunter just like his father Scott. But Scott did not like that, Angel would go to the forest along with John for hunting, but Adele was okay with the idea of Angel to learn how to hunt in the wild.

It was a month of July. The summer heat had toned down a little as rainfall became a daily routine. Adele left for Savannah to see her father who was not feeling well. He developed an edema on the heart that caused chest pain and discomfort in breathing.

She said, "I will stay there in Savannah for some time until my father feels better."

Scott felt he was free again from all restrictions imposed by his wife. He became drunk and cursed everybody around one evening and picked a fight with John and went to the fieldhouse looking for Martha. When he found Martha, he cursed her and hit her with the walking cane he was using to support his limping gait. Angel was close by and he ran after Scott to stop him from hitting Martha. Scott was furious and cursed Angel with all his hatred towards him. Angel was furious seeing his father hurting his mama. Scott called Angel names and struck him with his cane and said, "You white nigger, I will kill you."

Angel pushed Scott on the floor, kicked him in his

stomach and subdued his father. John ran toward Scott and protected him from Angel's rage. All this happened within an hour with no provocation or expected trouble. Plantation overseer John along with the help of other slaves took Scott to his bungalow and cleaned him with warm water so that Scott could come out from the influence of liquor and become sober. All this commotion and the effects of alcohol and physical strain made Scott exhausted, so he laid down in his bed and fell asleep.

The next morning Scott got up early and dressed up to ride his white horse. He opened his study and picked up his favorite Henry rifle from the gun rack and inserted .44 caliber cartridges in the rifle and locked the chamber. Scott galloped his horse to the forest a few miles from his plantation and headed to the next plantation about ten miles away. Henry Smith was the owner of the other plantation. Scott knew that Angel often visited Mr. Smith's plantation because he had a daughter named Camelia who Angel liked. While riding, Scott hatched a plan how to kill Angel, because he felt that Angel humiliated him and kicked him in front of everybody and took away his pride as the owner of the plantation and the slaves.

In his mind Scott envisioned the plan he could execute with nobody knowing he planned to kill Angel. His plan involved a scenario where Scott would act as a drunk and curse everybody around including Angel and Martha. Then he would poke Martha with his cane that would bring Angel to the spot to save his mama from a beating. At that moment Scott would pull out his Colt Dragon revolver from the gun belt and point it at Angel's head. Angel would react to get away from the pistol and most probably try to grab Scott's hand so that the pistol will be pointed in another direction. During the scuffle the pistol would discharge hitting Angel and killing him. Scott would act like he did not put bullets in the revolver but Angel did. Everybody in the plantation knew Angel liked to hunt and used guns often during his hunting trips in the forest with John.

Scott felt proud of his plan to kill Angel. He never liked him because Angel was close to Martha and black children growing up with them. He was waiting for the right moment to execute and accomplish his desire to eliminate Angel from his life.

A few weeks passed by. Adele's father's health went downhill and he died after suffering a massive heart attack while sleeping in his bed in the night. Scott had to go to Savannah to mourn his father-in-law's sudden demise.

Two weeks after his father-in-law's death Scott came back to his plantation alone without his wife Adele. Adele stayed in Savannah and took care of her ailing mother. After her father's death she realized that her mother also would follow soon in her father's footsteps and leave her alone in this world. She was fond of her father and mother and wanted to spend the remaining days with her mother, taking care of her.

Scott was thrilled that Adele stayed with her mother. He never liked Adele because he believed in a marriage where a husband should have all the privileges of free, unattached freedom and to enjoy the life with alcohol, women, and fornication. Adele followed the Puritan philosophy and religious beliefs. She received an education at home and was quite an intelligent woman. She never accepted Scott's volatile personality, womanizing behavior, and prohibited Scott's philandering behavior. She could not bear a child and she felt that life had betrayed her so she took God as her salvation and followed that path.

Adele's absence gave Scott a new life of heavy drinking and abuse of power groping young girls. Everybody avoided Scott in the evening when he was intoxicated with liquor. It was a Friday evening in September, Scott was drunk and his gait was unstable. He had arrived at the fieldhouse carrying his favorite Henry rifle with him. He looked for Martha and found her in the kitchen. He cursed her. At this point Angel came out and stood before Scott and said, "You are drunk; leave this place and stop cursing people."

Scott said, "Who are you to tell me I am drunk?"

Angel moved forward towards Scott and said, "Please Papa go to your bungalow and rest."

Scott was very surprised to hear Angel's calm voice calling him Papa. For a few seconds Scott was speechless but his drunken condition brought a sense of uncontrolled rage towards Angel and he shouted, "I am not your Papa. You are a white nigger" and pointed the gun at his throat.

Angel realized that Scott was drunk and could kill him. A scuffle ensued. In a split second Angel moved his neck away from the gun and grabbed the muzzle of the rifle and raised it above his head, so that if the gun goes off then the bullet would fly above his head and cause no harm. Scott pulled the trigger and a bullet flew above Angel's head and hit the wall before ricocheting into the kitchen table. To save himself from Scott's murderous intent, Angel kicked the left leg which suffered the horse's kick many years ago. Scott's left foot slipped because of Angel's kick and Scott lost his balance and dropped the rifle on the ground.

The gun fell vertically on the ground and the impact caused the gun to discharge its ammunition. A bullet hit Scott in the neck. Scott fell on top of the rifle and blood flowed.

Martha shouted at John the overseer and asked him please fetch the doctor from the town. She ran and collected a clean rag and placed it over the wound and held it with pressure so that the bleeding would stop.

John jumped on horseback and galloped as fast he could to fetch the doctor from the town. Within an hour John brought Dr. Richardson with him to the fieldhouse. He looked at Scott and examined him. He cleaned the wound with boiled water and stitched his wound and wrapped the area with cotton pads. Richardson realized that Scott had lost an enormous amount of blood and he could not save his life.

Around midnight Dr. Richardson pronounced Scott dead. Angel wrapped around his dad's body and a high-pitched crying voice came out of his throat. That sound echoed in the room and a moaning sound asked, "Why, why are you leaving me Papa?"

The news of Scott's death reached surrounding plantations and the small town. The sheriff Jack Monroe came to Scott's plantation and asked people how Scott got shot. Everybody told the sheriff that Scott's gun accidentally misfired and hit his neck that killed him. The sheriff was not interested in listening to what plantation slaves told him because he knew that slaves' testimony had no value in the court and would not be accepted by the law of Georgia. So he locked Angel in the jail for murdering Scott King.

Martha pleaded with the sheriff that Angel had nothing to do in this incident and should not be kept in the jail. The sheriff said, "Let the Judge decide. Until then I will keep him in the jail."

Rumors flew regarding Scott's death. Somebody said Angel killed Scott because witch Martha gave a potion that changed Angel's disposition and was responsible for killing Scott. The Sheriff sent a telegram to the Sheriff's office in Savannah so they could contact Adele and inform her of her husband's death. Adele took a horse driven carriage and headed for Vienna to come home.

It was a beautiful autumn day; the sun was up but passing clouds embraced the sun off and on and played peekaboo. They locked Angel in the jail as Sheriff Monroe wanted. The Sheriff said, "I am keeping Angel in the jail for his own safety and protecting him from the crowd until his trial in the courthouse following week."

The Sheriff allowed nobody to see Angel except Adele. She came back to her home as fast as possible so she could take possession of Scott's business enterprise and financial interest. She was never close to Scott and disliked his amorous adventures and drunken states. Also, Adele blamed Scott for not having a child from their union because of his excessive philandering and alcohol abuse.

Adele asked Angel why he killed Scott. Angel told her it was an accident and he did nothing to hurt his father. Instead he tried to take the gun away from Scott's hand so that Scott would hurt nobody including himself because he was drunk, under the spell of alcohol.

Adele said, "God will punish you for your sin and you will rot in hell."

She showed her hatred towards Angel outwardly but deep down she was very contented because now she would be the one to control and own the profitable plantation. Money and power could corrupt people and could transform a person into a being who became addicted to power and control over their subordinates and a blind soul filled with arrogance, hate, indifference, and a purveyor of injustice.

The county courthouse was situated in the middle of the town. It was a nondescript building surrounded by two other buildings including the jailhouse and county offices. The circuit court judge was a middle-aged white man named Stephen Honeycutt who had been running the business of the county courthouse like a bulldog. He did not allow any indiscretion, any kind of commotion or disturbance in the court. Everybody around the county was scared of the judge because he was famous for putting people in hard labor for the maximum punishment allowed in the book.

They set the trial of Angel on Monday at 10 am. The county courthouse was filled with people. The whites were clustered in one side of the courthouse and the blacks sat on the opposite side of the courthouse. Outside of the courthouse white folks were attending a carnival, as many hawkers gathered around the courthouse selling their stuff. The majority of the whites gathered there were discussing the fate of Angel and whether or not he would receive a guilty verdict. The judge selected jurors from people who lived in the town and all the jurors were white.

The slaves could not be a juror according to state laws. Blacks had no power to influence the outcome of the legal proceedings. They were the silent observer and recipient of white injustice all the time.

Even though Angel was a hundred percent white, but he was raised and nurtured to health by a black woman because of death of his mother, many white neighbors considered him black. His father Scott never liked him and most of the time hurled abusive and derogatory insults for no reason. Martha acted as his mother and protected Angel from abusive treatment. Often Scott was drunk, and he beat Martha, called her names just because she gave absolute love and affection and care to Angel.

The county prosecutor McDougall was a short, tobacco chewing, barrel shaped white man age sixty. The State selected a local solicitor for Angel named Michael Douglas who had little courtroom experience as a defense attorney. This selection of an inexperienced solicitor for Angel was a sign that the county believed that Angel killed his father deliberately and must be guilty of the crime.

It was a balmy morning. The sun was bright. The courthouse was jam-packed. When the clock reached 10 am the court clerk entered the center of the room and said in a solemn voice, "Please rise."

The Hon. Judge Honeycutt entered the chamber and said, "Please be seated."

The courtroom chamber was spacious, a rectangular shaped area. The judge's table faced east, the spectators' gallery faced north and south and the jury box was situated close to the judge's table. The county solicitor and defense attorney along with the defendant shackled in a chain were seated facing the judge. Seven jurors, all white males, were seated in the box facing the judge. Judge Honeycutt asked prosecutor McDougal to present the case in front of public and the jury. McDougal got up from his chair and said, "The defendant Angel King pulled the gun on Mr. Scott King who was drunk and physically unstable. The defendant intentionally kicked this unstable man so he could take the gun away from him and then pulled the trigger to kill Mr. Scott King.

The judge asked, "Mr. McDougal do you have any

witnesses who can provide detailed information about this incident?"

"Your honor, I will present Mr. John Cummings to the court. Mr. Cummings is the overseer of the plantation and he was present during this incident."

Mr. Cummings stepped forward to the witness stand and the court clerk swore him in as the witness and he raised his right hand and said, "I shall tell the whole truth, nothing but the truth, so help me God."

Mr. McDougal asked Mr. Cummings to tell the jury what happened in the field house during the evening hours of September 13.

"It was around seven o'clock in the evening I was talking to David our field driver in front of the field house. I heard the loud voice of Mr. King coming from the field house and I rushed toward the field house and entered the veranda. I noticed that many slave women were watching a scuffle between Master Scott King and his son Angel King. Both men were trying to pull the rifle away from the other person. Then suddenly a loud sound came out as the trigger was pulled. A bullet hit the brick wall and ricocheted off the wall and pierced the wooden frame of the table and was embedded in it."

Mr. Cummings paused for a few seconds, then continued to describe what was happening in the field house. "The scuffle continued between father and son. Mr. King's hands were close to the butt of the rifle and close to the chamber of the barrel while Angel was holding the muzzle of the rifle.

"Suddenly, Angel kicked Mr. Scott in the left leg that made Master Scott lose his balance and drop the rifle on the floor of the veranda."

Mr. Cummings became silent. The judge with his

commanding voice shattered the silence and said, "Mr. Cummings please continue your testimony."

"Yes, your honor."

Drops of sweat covered the face of Mr. Cummings. He took a deep breath and said, "The rifle fell on the brick floor and discharged the bullet with a tremendous thud. At the same time Mr. King fell on top of the rifle."

Mr. Cummings sat there for a few seconds and tried to compose his thoughts. Then he said, "I saw blood gushing out from Mr. King's neck.

"Martha screamed at me and said, 'John take the horse and get Dr. Richardson as fast as possible."

"I jumped from the veranda and run out of the field house to the stable to collect a colt and galloped as fast as I could."

Mr. Cummings continued his testimony and said, "Within an hour I brought Dr. Richardson with me and entered the fieldhouse. Martha with the help of other slaves placed Mr. King on the bed and she covered the wound with layers of rags and pressing wound area with her hand to stop bleeding. The doctor removed the rags and cleaned the wound with warm water and stitched the wound in the neck. Then placed many layers of cotton pads and bandage the area with cheesecloth."

Mr. McDougal asked Mr. Cummings, "What was Mr. Angel King was doing at this time?"

Mr. Cummings said, "Mr. Angel King was moaning and saying, "Why are you leaving me Papa? Why?"

Mr. McDougal told the judge he has no more questions to ask Mr. Cummings.

The judge asked the defense counsel Mr. Michael Douglas to proceed with his cross-examination of the witness.

Mr. Douglas came forward and stood in front of Mr.

Cummings and asked, "Who owned the rifle used in the shooting on 13 September evening?"

"The rifle belonged to Mr. Scott King," answered Mr. Cummings.

"Mr. Cummings, you testified earlier that during the scuffle between Mr. Scott King and Angel King the defendant kicked Mr. Scott King which forced elder King to lose his balance and drop the rifle on the floor. Is this statement correct?"

"Yes, the statement is correct."

"When the rifle hit the brick floor and discharged the ammunition, was there any physical connection between the defendant and the rifle?" asked Mr. Douglas.

"What do you mean by the physical connection between Angel King and the rifle, Mr. Douglas?" said Mr. Cummings.

"Let me try to simplify the question. Did the rifle while falling to the ground have any physical contact/control with the defendant? Please answer yes or no."

"No," said Mr. Cummings.

"Was there any physical control of the rifle by the defendant? Please answer yes or no."

"No," said Mr. Cummings.

"In other words, Mr. Cummings you are convinced that Mr. Angel King had no physical possession of the rifle when it slipped from the hand of Mr. Scott King, and fell to the ground."

"Objection, your Honor, the defense counsel is trying to influence the witness with his own ideas."

"Sustained. Counsel please refrain from influencing the witness with your own convictions," said the judge.

"Yes, your Honor," said Douglas.

"Would you agree to the fact that neither Mr. Scott King nor Angel King had control of the rifle, when it slipped out of Mr. Scott King's hand, and fell to the ground? Please answer the court yes or no," asked Mr. Douglas.

"Yes," said Mr. Cummings.

"Mr. Cummings would you agree to the fact that the rifle misfired when it hit the ground and neither Scott King nor Angel King controlled the event."

Mr. Cummings hesitated and kept silent. The judge roared, "Please answer the question Mr. Cummings."

"Yes," a feeble answer came from Mr. Cummings.

Mr. Douglas said, "The rifle fired accidentally when it hit the ground and neither Scott King nor Angel King had any control of the event."

"Objection, your honor. The counsel is telling the witness what to say."

"Objection overruled," said the judge.

"Your honor, I have no more questions to ask Mr. Cummings," said Douglas.

Both the lawyers agreed that they had concluded their argument and requested the judge for jury deliberation and the verdict thereof.

The judge instructed the jury to go through the evidence presented and make a decision based on their analysis of the facts and conclude based on their honest and thoughtful interpretations. The judge ordered a recess.

The jury moved to an adjacent room and locked the door. They were busy deliberating and deciding whether Mr. Angel King was guilty of committing a murder or not guilty of the charges levied upon him.

After an hour the foreman of the jury notified the court

that the jury had completed their deliberation and reached a decision in this case. The clerk of the court notified the judge about the decision and the judge asked the court to resume the proceedings. The judge entered the courtroom and sat in his chair. He asked the foreman of the jury to come forward and deliver the jury's decision to him. Judge Honeycutt read the jury report and announced each individual juror's decision one by one in the court.

The decision was unanimous, "Not guilty!"

A commotion broke out in the courtroom. The judge screamed, "Order! Order! I will charge anybody who defies the order in this courtroom with contempt of the court and put them into jail."

The judge's outburst and threat brought immediate silence in the court.

Judge Honeycutt pronounced, "Mr. Angel King is not guilty of murdering Mr. Scott King. However, Mr. Angel King violated social order in the fieldhouse of King Plantation on 13 September evening. For this violation, I will place Mr. Angel King in the jail for a term of six months beginning today after these proceedings." The judge adjourned the court.

The town was divided on hearing the verdict "not guilty". All the slaves were thrilled because Angel was spared a death sentence by hanging. Martha cried and thank the Lord for saving her child, Angel. Many occasions Martha wondered why she had to suffer so much so she could be alive. She lost her husband Solomon and the baby whom Scott sold off to traders, enormous beatings and inhuman torture from Scott King just because of her love, affection and dedication towards Angel.

Most whites were happy to see Angel avoid a death

sentence but quite a few white supremacists believed that Angel murdered his father Scott and should be hanged in the middle of the town. Adele was neutral in this matter. She had no opinion about Angel's culpability in Scott King's death. Her main interest was to inherit the property after Scott's death. Angel King was standing as the barrier against the desire of Adele's wicked schemes.

Two weeks went by. It was December in Dooly County, Georgia. The cool air pierced the stillness of the morning. The sun opened its eye and flooded the land below with his radiant bright sunrays that sparkled on the ice crystal covered blades of grasses and the naked branches of the pecan trees that greeted it with happiness and said, "Welcome and good morning."

Cool air danced with the grasses with no inhibition or control. It was a wonderful morning.

Angel was locked up in a solitary cell large enough to hold a single cot, a pillow filled with dry hay and a rag as a blanket to cover the body. Angel got used to the harsh condition in the jail and counted every day to get out of this hell. Martha visited twice; she cried. Tears rolled over her cheeks like an endless spout which did not know how to stop the flow. Angel with his sparkling eyes consoled her and said, "Mama, have faith in God; He will make me free." Martha silently shed her tears!

It was the 10th of December. In the middle of night Angel heard a noise of the opening of the iron gate of his cell and someone grabbed his neck and placed a jute bag over his face. It was very dark. Angel struggled to free himself and make a noise but his mouth was shut tightly with a rag; only a groan came out from his lungs. He felt he could not breathe anymore and became unconscious.

When Angel regained consciousness, he found himself tied to a tree. They tied his hands to the branches of a naked tree just as Jesus Christ hung on a cross. He realized that he would be lynched by the mob and hanged. A cold shiver passed along his spinal column but he could not feel any pain in his body. It appeared the body shut down the sensation of pain as if death touched his body and drank all the sensibilities from him, so that death could carry him into his kingdom and anoint him the ultimate freedom he was seeking for a long time.

A large mob gathered in the center of the town near the jail. Sheriff Monroe and his people were nowhere as if they did not exist in this town. Around 10 o'clock a group of men carrying rifles came close to the naked tree where Angel's body was hoisted. The leader of the group known as the Dragon said, "Peoples Justice found Angel King murdered his father Scott King in cold blood and he is a Negro loving white Nigger, who must die by hanging for his lapse of Christian values and undermining the superiority of white race. A man born white must follow the basic tenet of racial purity and superiority."

Then Dragon asked Angel if he wanted to repent of his sin and ask for forgiveness.

Angel King mustered all his strength and said, "whites believe that they are the chosen people by the disciple of God and rule the world. They chained and tortured Negroes for their own interest of profit-making endeavor, treated them as savages in the name of Christian God. Whites wrapped around them with the cloak of religious piety and profess universality of God's existence but denying the multitude of humanity the basic tenet of living in peace and prosperity. Oh, what a pity! All these sacraments they profess are nothing but a great lie!

The human life is precious, but in the name of religious purity they have decimated millions and stole everything from them. Is this the face of God? Or a deceitful image of profit-making self-interest!"

Someone pulled the pedestal on which rested Angel's feet. The noose snapped tightly on the neck of Angel and choked him to death. A faint smile lingered on Angel's face as he left the mortal body and joined the journey towards immortality!

BINA

The same routine everyday makes me angry. Sometimes I feel I must revolt from this boring and tiring life. There is nothing dynamic, only arduous, monotonous, and irksome happening as routinely as possible, like a damned clock that tics, tics, and tics. It is an unbearable, unbelievable, and intolerable situation. I cannot understand how life could be so dull and miserable. The living cannot be that boring. If that is the life then there is no need to be alive. Maybe death would be different; at least it will not be the 'same monotonous routine'! It will be something new, untasted and inexperienced.

I know all of you are wondering what I am talking about. Are you sure you would like to hear about me and my boring routine? I don't think so. If your life is full of actions, anecdotes or some interesting episodes, then you need not know about this ordinary life... Well are you still interested? I guess not. But I will take the liberty to tell you my humble story. It goes this way... I get up early in the morning around six o'clock, take a shower, eat my breakfast and read just the headlines from the newspaper and then I am ready to go to my office in Calcutta's famous Dalhousie Square. These days even the newspapers headlines are dull. Nothing interesting is happening anywhere in the world, even in Calcutta. Calcutta is the cradle of the revolutionaries. It is the capital of the processions and protest marches. It is the city where the revolution would start in India to eliminate the whole bourgeoisie society so that a proletariat regime would come and liberate anemic human corpses. But even there those revolutionaries only churn rhetoric under the smoke-filled cafes of the College Street. Now you see why I am so bored, hopeless and lifeless.

The same 8:15 train from Garia to Sealdah, every morning. The train is filled with human flesh; thin, fat, bald-headed or curly-haired men are everywhere. Women are also in the train sandwiched between men. Some men take advantage of this crowded condition and pinch those women to fulfil their unfulfilled desire through perverted and lewd manners. These female office workers don't mind this libidinous behavior because they know that it is one hazard of being alive and working. To have a job in this society is considered as the God's blessing on your life.

As usual I hang in there like a bat and pray to the Almighty to protect me from banging on those bloodthirsty electric posts. God listens to my prayer every day and I arrive at Sealdah safely. Once in Sealdah, I had to run for a tramcar which would take me to Dalhousie Square. Without my knowledge, I would arrive in my office as usual. The same crowded tram car, hanging in the train like a bat, that damned boring routine I follow at the end of the workday to reach my home, only in a different direction — in reverse! Undergoing this shocking, absurd and acrobatic feat every day causes my body to get into a routine and it has accepted this as the truth. Daily sore muscles even forgot how to protest. This is the price to pay for having a job in this jobless society. I feel I am lucky and have been chosen by the God for this clerical job.

On that day while coming out from the office my mind

revolted. I decided to take a walk along the bank of the river Ganges. I bought roasted peanuts, some spiced puffed rice and munched them to take away my hungry stomach. I walked for a while along the riverbank and then sat on a concrete chair beside the riverbank. High tide came with a tremendous gush and splashed the shore with a heavy gargling noise. The large ships started their siren, 'vu', 'vu', 'vu', like a well-fed man who burped with a loud noise, expressing his satisfaction.

Dusk set in. The light posts blinked their eyes for a second with fluorescent lights before their permanent glow. At that moment, I felt it would have been better if I were a lamp post. On the other side of the river a chain of smoke curled up in the sky through the chimneys of the jute mills, like a formless body of a dancer vanished in emptiness. Gypsy women were hunting for the prey in the shadow of darkness. A masseur tossed a line while passing by my site, "Girl sir, exquisite sir, very sexy."

I looked at the sky with disgust. It was grayish, filled with clouds. I got up from the chair and walked toward Dalhousie Square. On my way, I saw a beggar sitting under a light post. He took out a small cloth sack filled with money from his waist band tucked under and rested it on the side of his left leg. Then with absolute love and tenderness he petted his bloody, open leprotic wound, and with a serene gratitude saluted the Allah for this wonderful gift...

My mind was filled with a strange experience. I felt I was mature and had some special meaning in my life, besides my responsibility to Bina. Under this exceptional dark night, I realized I was happy. I was alive, well and had a family. My own Bina, the motherless daughter was waiting for me at home. She was worried, restless and might be frightened.

Perhaps she was crying for me and praying to God for my safety. She knew my routine. For her that routine was happiness.

I ran. A serene contentment filled my body and mind. I was in a peaceful bliss. I looked at the sky. The shadow of the cloud cleared up, and the moon smiled at me with her soft glitter just like my little Bina...

MAGDA

Richard Smith, CEO of Smith Enterprise, lifted the window blind from his window seat to see the weather outside as the plane landed in Budapest airport. It was a cloudy day, fog spread its veil, as if a maiden covering her face from the onlookers. Richard hailed a taxicab to go to his hotel, Novotel, in the heart of Budapest. He wanted to lie down for some time, so he could catch a short nap before he headed to his meeting with his partners in Budapest.

The room was spacious. At the center of the room there was a small table with a leather sofa next to it. A wall clock, a somewhat vintage type, kept time with an oscillating pendulum reminding of a vestige of the old Hungarian communist regime.

The sound of a ringing phone broke the silence of the slumber that engulfed Richard in a dream state. He lifted the headset to answer the phone. "Hello."

"Hi Richard, this is Boris. How was your flight?"

"It was great. I just fell asleep for a while."

"Good, take a rest today. Tomorrow we will go to the office. I will pick you up from your hotel at 9:30 am."

"Thanks Boris; see you tomorrow."

Richard looked at the room. His sleepy eyes rolled like a video camera, focused on each item of the room for a few seconds, then moved on to the next item. The bed, sofa, table, chair, closet, bathroom and other inanimate objects were there for use. Nothing interested him except that old vintage wall clock. That swinging pendulum with a red metal ball at the end somehow attracted his eyes. He fixed his eyes on the clock. That tic-toc mesmerized him. He felt that clock was telling him something but what was it saying? Richard fell asleep again.

Boris came to pick up Richard from his hotel and took him to his office which was located in the best section of the town. The multi-storied building housed many offices including Boris's company which built houses around Budapest. An office door with a gold metal tablet read 509, Boris Sharkasky Construction. Boris rang the doorbell, and a blonde wearing a black suite opened the door.

"Hi Monika, this is Richard Smith."

"Good morning. It is a pleasure to meet you. Please come in."

At the center of the conference room was a square table with six chairs around the table. They decorated the windows with golden curtains. Through the window one could see the majestic Danube River flowing fast. Recent rain swelled the river and that increased the flow of water. The chain bridge was close by. Lions guarded the entrance of the bridge which connected the city of Buda with Pest.

The meeting lasted for two hours as they discussed the strategy, finance, government policies and politics, building regulatory practices, and other business-related matters. After a long day's work Boris suggested that Richard needed some relaxation — a visit to a spa. Budapest was world famous for its wonder spas.

Boris took Richard to Golden Triangle, his favorite spa in Budapest. An usher led Richard to a room and asked him to be seated and left the room. The room was decorated with bluish wallpaper. One twin bed was in the center of the room. One side of the wall had a stack of white towels. A little fountain stood in one corner of the room. The other corner of the room had a hydrothermal furnace shaped like a triangle holding lava stones. Dim bluish florescent light canopied the room; the gurgling sound of flowing water in the corner fountain created an illusionary ambience where time and space intertwined into a panorama of stillness. Light fragrance from a burning incense floated in a dance of expectation. The velvet curtain of the door opened slightly. Richard could see a woman covered with a see-through chiffon robe inside. She asked Richard to disrobe and lay down on the bed. Her face was covered with a silk veil. She caressed Richard's shoulder and neck with gentle strokes, then placed warm lava stones on pressure points. Richard felt a wonderful warmth emanating from the stones that energized his whole body, mind, and whole being. He was in a blissful state, where peace, serenity, and silence purified your essence of life — the existence!

Richard noticed that the silk veil shifted its place and exposed the woman's face and bright eyes that twinkled like stars. Those shining bright eyes in a dimly lit room created a thunderbolt in the mind of Richard. He screamed, "Stop! Please stop!"

The woman pulled her veil and moved away from Richard and said in a soft voice, "It is okay, I will not hurt you."

"Please leave the room," said Richard. He was disturbed and perplexed. The woman left the room. Richard sat there on the bed for a while and tried to settle down from this unusual experience.

The next day Boris asked Richard how he liked the spa

experience. Richard said, "I liked it a lot. It was a great experience."

Boris grinned a lot and said in a mischievous tone, "Enjoy Budapest because it is the best place on earth to get these experiences."

Richard showed a faint smile and asked Boris, "Please find out the name of the woman who was with me last night."

Boris laughed loudly and said, "Oh, you have already found the woman of your dream!" Richard replied, with a serious tone, "Yes, I have."

Boris was a regular customer of Golden Triangle, and he had a good connection with the owner of the place. He found out the name of the woman who served Richard that night. He called Richard and said, "Her name is Magda and she's a gypsy."

Richard thanked Boris and asked him if Magda could see him in his hotel. Boris said, "Yes if the price is right".

Richard told Boris, "Please ask Magda to see me in my hotel tomorrow night."

It was Tuesday evening. Richard was anxiously waiting for Magda to come to his hotel room. Boris made all the arrangements for this meeting. Richard was nervous and could not focus on anything. He felt that the time stood still and was not moving forward. He sat on a chair in the room looking at the clock to see if the pendulum was oscillating or not. Perspiration covered his forehead and he went through an anxiety attack.

The florescent light was bright but a stale air in the room prevailed. Richard got up from his chair and spaced up and down the room. The clock was ticking just to encourage

Richard that time was flowing forward and it would soon fulfil the expectation. The telephone rang. Richard picked up the phone and said, "Hello."

"This is from the front desk; a visitor is waiting for you in the lobby."

"Thank you. I'll be there in a minute," said Richard.

Richard looked at his wristwatch and the time was 8 pm.

Richard took the elevator and reached the lobby. He found Magda sitting in a sofa next to the grand piano. Richard moved towards the sofa and greeted Magda with a smile and said, "Hi Magda. Thank you for coming."

Magda extended her hand to greet him. Her hand was cold, and she showed a slight fear in her eyes.

Richard escorted Magda to his suite. He asked her to sit on the loveseat sofa, which was occupying the room's corner, next to the window. Magda sat on the sofa without uttering a word; only her bright eyes showed a shade of gloom or uneasiness.

Richard poured some Cointreau in a glass and handed to her. She softly said, "Thank you."

Richard's eyes were scanning Magda's features. She was about eighteen to twenty years of age, petite about 5'3" tall, dark green eyes mixed with a hue of brown, glittering like a full moon. She was wearing a bluish jumpsuit with black high heel shoes and holding a blue purse with a golden border.

The room was silent only the sound of the clock; Tick-Tock telling that time was moving forward as usual.

The Cointreau gave a little boost to Magda, and she asked Richard, "What kind of service would you like to have?"

Richard did not answer. He fixed his eyes on Magda's bright greenish eyes. He was not there, perhaps somewhere in

69

a distant land dreaming the impossible dream.

Magda stood up from the sofa, unbuttoned her blouse, came close to Richard's bed where he was lying down and asked him, "What type of service do you desire?"

Richard answered, "Please button your blouse, and sit here on the bed."

It surprised Magda to hear the answer. She wondered if she heard correctly.

In disbelief Magda again asked Richard, "Am I not good enough for you? Why did you ask me to come to your hotel tonight?"

Richard said, "I asked you to come so you could tell me your story."

It puzzled Magda. She knew men only wanted sex. They were like animals who wanted to devour human flesh and proclaim superiority over women.

In her profession, Magda had never come across a man who did not want her to perform a sexual act. Richard asked Magda to sit beside him in the bed, and said, "Tell me everything about you, where were you born, your childhood growing up, and your dreams."

Magda in her mind thought this man was a strange and unusual human being. He paid a lot of money just to hear her story. It was unreal! This man must be crazy and she better leave this room and the man. In her short life, she had experienced men in different shades; some were sex-starved beast, some were perverts and hedonistic, some were sheer brutes but this man was so different. He was soft as a feather and he reminded her of her father. She reminisced about her childhood, growing up in the village.

Richard asked Magda again to tell him her story.

Magda opened up to tell her story. In a melancholy voice she said, "My mother died when I was fourteen years old. We worked on a farm as a sharecropper. The owner of the land allowed us to grow wheat, corn, and other vegetables. Every year we had to give the landowner half of the crops we grew in the land, and the other half we could keep for our own use. We had to buy seeds and fertilizers from him on credit, which often put us more in debt and the owner forced my dad Mihal to sign papers that made our whole family as indentured laborers until we paid back our debts." Magda looked at Richard with tears in her eyes. Richard held her hand and said, "Everything will be all right."

She continued her story. "Since my mother's death, I helped my dad in the field. I also tended the landowner's flock of lamb every day. One afternoon when we were in the fields my dad had a heart attack, and he became paralyzed in one side of his body. That was the time I felt, God took away everything from us. He took away my mother from me, then now he took away my father, only leaving me to suffer the anguish and uncertainty of my life. Why? What did I do to deserve this punishment? Is it because I am alive and I exist?" Magda looked at Richard with tears in his eyes.

Richard held her hand and said, "Everything will be all right. Don't blame yourself. You have done nothing wrong."

Richard's gentle, affectionate touch and warm feelings towards Magda brought solace to this beautiful girl. The silence engulfed Magda and Richard in a spell of serenity. Only the clock kept interrupting the silence. Richard asked Magda to come back the following night.

Magda was happy; at the same time, she was not sure how to categorize Richard as a person. He was a warm, sympathetic, and sensitive human being with many fine qualities and character. He believed in tenderness and affection. Magda developed a bond, a connection, and respect where humanity could flourish.

Magda arrived at Richard's hotel and gave him a small gift. Richard was happily surprised and accepted the gift. Magda asked Richard, "Please open the box."

Richard opened the box and found a small butterfly pin. Richard was very excited to receive the pin and said, "I always wanted to have a butterfly pin for my jacket. How could you read my mind?

It is a telepathic connection."

Magda was contented to see Richard happy. Magda continued her story. She said, "My father's health deteriorated; he almost became an invalid. The landlord Vasile demanded more money but there was no money left to give. Vasile suggested to my father that he send Magda to Budapest, where she could get a job in the spa and earn a lot of money.

"My father did not know what to say. The landowner Vasile said, "I know a person who could help Magda get a job in Budapest."

Father had no choice but accepted the offer from the landowner to let me work in Budapest.

"The following week Vasile sent a man known as Gabor to our house. A young lady named Maria was with Gabor. My father Mihal held my hand and said, "Magda, I love you dear. You are my soul. May Sarah Kali protect you from all evil spirits and bad men? I am an invalid and have no place to go; only death would bring me freedom. I am counting the days when that day would come and knock at my door and they take me away with him. This separation is so painful that it freezes my tears. They cannot flow — only my heart struggling to beat just to keep me alive, so I can suffer this pain. This anguish and hopelessness must give happiness to mighty God, who forgot how to take away the pain from a dying man, so that some peace can come to this wretched soul."

"Papa don't say these things. Sarah Kali will protect me. She will make you strong and help you get better. I will come often to see you. I love you." Magda shed no tears only determination filled her persona with resilience and acceptance to this inevitable fate.

Gabor's girlfriend Maria was a twenty-five-year-old. She took the role of an older sister to Magda, and explained how the spa business ran, what people expected from the girls who were attending the clients who came to unwind from their stressful life in the spa. Maria was nice to Magda, and all three lived in a rundown apartment next to the Jewish section of Buda.

Gabor worked for an underground company whose main business was to recruit girls from poor Romania peasants and Hungary to bring them to Budapest and force them to work in the spa industry, where young girls entertained the customers coming from all over the world. Young girls received training in massage therapy and other techniques that could relax and release tension from the rich clients willing to pay hefty fees for these services.

Gabor had an evil eye on Magda. He wanted to seduce her, but Maria always kept an eye on Gabor, and protected Magda from Gabor's lust.

One night in the spa a rich American businessman came to Golden Triangle and wanted an erotic massage. He was looking for a young girl to provide this service. The manager

Anghel asked Magda to do this special favor and attend this man. Magda reluctantly went to serve the man's need.

Magda gave him the chocolate massage, where the massaging oil contained pure cocoa, cocoa oil, and theobromine mixture, which bought an intense sensual and revitalizing feeling. During the massage the man grabbed Magda and raped her. She did not scream, only suffered this vicious animalistic violation of her womanhood. That monster stole her innocence! Now Magda was in a profession where money was everything — there was no value of decency, love, or humanity. Just like a robot, you could earn a living without feeling or emotion. The life lost its innocence!

Magda told Maria what happened in the spa. Both held each other. Only silence and a stream of tear drops rolled down the cheeks of both the sisters in melancholy. There were no one to help Magda in this brutality. Police and other law enforcement agency would not heed Magda's plea; instead they would punish Magda for staying in Budapest with no legal documents as they were refugees. Many undocumented young women lived in the city of glitter and opulence under the canopy of darkness, as non-existing human slaves serving people of wealth in this carnal industry.

Magda arrived at Richard's hotel in the evening. Richard asked her, "I want to hear the stories about the fireflies." It was a full moon; the moon was shining on the waves of the Danube. Magda was happy and she started a story.

"We lived in a small house in the middle of farmland where a flock of sheep wandered around this village close to Chino Valley where the River Mures flows. The river formed many branching tributaries along our village. In the summer when the water was low, we took a bath in the Little River and sometimes we washed our clothes in the river.

"In the evening sometimes, I spread a small blanket close to the riverbank and looked at the distant stars, wondering why they twinkled in the sky. Sometimes, I found fireflies dancing around the creek blinking their glow to call their partners to come close by. Each flash of light from a female firefly attracted a male firefly. Then they danced in unison. This dance of light flashed in the depth of darkness, making me feel if I were a firefly, I could dance like them. During the full moon, the whole field beamed with light. Sometimes passing clouds played hide and seek with the moonlight creating an illusion of light and darkness.

"In the close by swamps sudden flashes of light appeared from the bottom of the muddy bogs. The flash of light lingered in a wavy hue and disappeared. Again, it reappeared from another spot further from the original site. In the moonlight, I danced alone as a maiden who had drank nectar of wildflowers with no inhibition, as an *Opsora* to please the goddess of love.

"I caught some fireflies with a fishnet and made a firefly lantern in which to place them. I hung the lantern on a tree branch and looked at them in the night. They were my pets, but they were not thrilled because I did not see them flashing their glowing glory. Within a week they died. I realized that fireflies flashed their light only when they were free. Freedom was their life. If that was taken away, they refused to live, because for them once freedom was lost there was nothing left for them.

"A few weeks later, I caught more fireflies with my fishnet and placed them in my lantern filled with wet grasses and mosses. One night I opened the lantern so the fireflies could escape. Once the little door of the lantern opened a firefly jumped out from the leaf filled lantern; it fluttered its wings just in front of me and then I saw her underbelly glowing like a hearth. Other fireflies extracted themselves from the lantern and flashed. They formed a circle around me and flashed their underbellies. I could see the smile of fireflies sparkle in the deep darkness of the night."

One night, Magda asked Richard, "You have to tell me your story. I have told you everything I could think of. Now it is your turn. Are you sick?" Richard hesitated. He did not want to divulge anything about his personal life. Then he said, "I will tell you next week when we meet again."

Magda wondered. She wanted to know what Richard wanted.

A week passed by. No word from Richard. Magda wondered what happened to Richard. Why didn't he call her for a week? Was he sick? She missed him, but she knew that in this business flesh and money ruled the world. Emotion, affection and humanity did not exist!

Almost two weeks passed by. Magda tried many times to contact Richard in his hotel and nobody was there to answer his phone. One day the main desk answered her phone and said, "Mr. Richard Smith left the hotel."

Richard was gone forever. Magda thought about him all the time. He was a gentleman, an affectionate man who knew how to treat a lady and respect her. Always a question haunted Magda why Richard was so nice and kind to her. Why was he so different from all other men she came across in her adult life?

A month had gone by since Richard disappeared. An envelope

came to the spa bearing Magda's name. The manager handed the envelope to Magda. Magda's hand trembled when she saw the envelope coming from Richard, but there was no return address. She opened the envelope. There was a letter addressed to her. It read:

My dear Magda:

I hope this letter finds you healthy and well. I'm sorry that I had to leave Budapest without telling you goodbye. There is a reason for it. You insisted every day I should tell you my story. Now, I will tell you my story as promised.

Magda when I first saw you in the spa, I was shocked. Your sublime face and radiant innocence of your bright eyes mesmerized me. I was spellbound. Deep down in my memory there was a hidden fact that sprang out like an ankoor with a climax of Beethoven's Ninth Symphony. Magda you reminded me of my daughter Isabel. My wife divorced me fifteen years ago and took away custody of Isabel from me. I fought very hard to keep her with me. But a court order sealed my fate. I was deprived of my daughter. My wife took all my money and happiness because Isabel was not there with me. My world fell into pieces. Then time showed me how to get back with my life — I built my life again. Money and other objects I have enough, but my heart is empty. My first look at you in the spa, I realized that my daughter was back — my eyes welled up with tears.

Your story of life, your innocence made me feel I am living. You have given me the serenity I wanted in my life. I know your presence will be short in my life, but I know you have given me the strength to live. I will cherish this all my life until death. Here is a bank draft/check of €100,000 for you so you can pay off all debts and be free yourself from Vasile, the landowner. Love, Richard.

Tears flowed from Magda's eyes and sparkled like bright stars in the sky...

SHELLY

Arriving at the apartment, I found a yellow envelope in my mailbox. It was from my lawyer's office. After ten long years of marriage, today everything was over. First came the separation and then the — ultimate — the divorce! Now it was final. I felt strange now, alone and lonely. The apartment was silent, like a stone house where even the wall lizards have forgotten to make their "tic, tic, tic," sound. Noises of my children were no longer there, only a deep sad silence. Solitude, loneliness and desolation hung around me like a creeping serpent... Wasn't this what I was looking for? Sometimes my wife's neurotic behavior, the children's noises, the telephone and the television's constant bombardments made me feel I was a prisoner, a prisoner by my family. I had no freedom. The yellow envelope told me that my freedom was here at last, but why was I not happy? Was it me? Life was funny. You dreamed, planned and worked so hard to get something you wanted, but when it was within your grasp, you found it had lost its appeal. It was the thing in life which would always be beyond your grasp that would taunt you forever. Without them you would be miserable. Even your existence would be in doubt.

My nagging loneliness forced me to go out of my apartment. I took the car and drove along Route 1. A young woman was standing on the side of the highway asking for a ride. Never had I given a ride to a stranger. I always avoided them. But my loneliness, my desolate existence made me change my usual habit. I stopped the car in front of her and signaled her to hop in. She smiled and got inside the car. I looked at her; she was in her early twenties. Wearing a tank top, which could barely hold in her white bosom, and tight shorts trying to cover her derriere... she was sexy!

She looked at me and asked, "Would you like to go to my place? We could have a good time together." I realized that she was a butterfly. I thought for a second and said, "I think that is a good idea."

"Fifty bucks, darling," she said.

She directed me to her apartment. We went inside. She asked me to take off my clothes and get comfortable on the bed. I did just that. I could not believe what was happening. A prostitute and me, oh what a combination! My education, pride, cultural background, all dumped in the gutter... that was too much; I stood up and tried to pull my pants on... but there she was, standing naked, her beautiful, voluptuous body. Her lusty and desirous look drew me closer to her body. I could not take it any more... I grabbed her flesh with passion, kissed her lips and sank myself within the softness of her pleasurable bliss...

Time passed, still half asleep, I heard a soft voice but could not recognize it. I saw a shadow beside me, a small, tiny figure with large eyes fixed on me. It surprised me. I was shocked, got up and in disbelief I saw a little girl standing beside my bed. She was looking at me with those piercing, innocent eyes. "Are you my daddy?" she asked. I shivered, could not say a word; I shook my head and said, "No, I am not your father."

She stared at me and said, "Why don't you want to be my daddy?"

I didn't know what to say. I was speechless… I was silent. I was, well I didn't know who I was. That look, that innocence… I stood up. I was afraid and restless. I wanted to scream and say, "I don't know you. I am not your daddy. I am nobody." But I lost all my strength. I was weak, tired and mute. She held me tightly with her tiny arms and said, "Daddy, stay with me. Don't go away. I need you."

I wanted to push her aside, but I did not have the strength. I looked at her. She was blonde with deep blue eyes which kept asking me in silence, "Why don't you want to be my father?"

Her look, those penetrating and innocent eyes, I could not take it anymore. It was too much. It was a torture, a torment! I remembered a few weeks ago I took my two children to the airport. Just before they boarded the plane, I saw the same look in their eyes. I closed my eyes, covered my ears, and screamed but no noise escaped from my vocal cords. They were frozen, atrophied, or non-existing. "Don't be afraid daddy. I am here, will protect you." I looked at her as tears rolled down my cheek. I picked her up and kissed her. Tears flowed over our merged cheeks and formed a stream of shining bubbles.

"Shelly, what are you doing? Sorry man I hope she didn't bother you. My daughter likes people. You know she wants to be close to people. OK baby, go back to the kitchen, in your bed." I put her down. She looked at me and said in a whisper, "Goodbye."

I retreated from the apartment and waved goodbye to those haunting eyes. That look… piercing and innocent… that living mirror of a life filled with love… that was existence. Human life will live as long as love exists. My empty life could not be empty. I had love, my children's love. Their life was my life. Their existence should nourish me through my existence. I had to live so they could live.

STORY OF A USELESS MAN AND HIS DOG

I pulled the car into the parking lot of Dr. Kenneth Newman, my primary care physician. It was Monday the fifth and my appointment was at 9:45 am; it was still fifteen minutes away. I signed my name in the front desk logbook and recorded the arrival time and appointment time. Then I sat on a chair, picked up a news magazine to read a few pages before Dr. Newman's nurse would call my name to go inside the examination room. Today's appointment was a six-month follow-up of my borderline diabetes and A1 C levels. I was a healthy person, no major complaints, except a past couple of months experiencing back pain, and slight tenderness on my rib cage.

Around 10 am Ashley, one of Dr. Newman's nurses called my name and guided me into examination room number three. She asked me to sit on the chair, took my blood pressure, pulse rate, body temperature and asked me about my back-pain threshold in the range from one to ten, where ten was the maximum pain. I answered her; it was about five.

She recorded all the information on my chart and said, "The doctor will be here in a few minutes" and then left the room.

A few minutes later Dr. Newman entered the room and said, "All your BP, A1 C, fasting sugar looked okay, but I want you to have an X-ray of your lumbar region and chest done within a week. I asked Ashley to make an appointment for you in the imaging center for X-rays and blood test in the clinical laboratory."

I asked Dr. Newman, "I just had blood work done a week ago. Why do I have to do more?"

He looked at me and said, "Pain in your back particularly, in the rib cage can become worse, as you are prone to arthritis and other stiff joint problems. I want to see if the bones are doing their job as they are supposed to do. Please come back next week."

Dr. Newman left the room. I felt a muscle spasm in my back which led me to a fear that something bad is coming my way. That fear was ephemeral, undefined and unexplainable.

The next day I went to the imaging centers, did an X-ray of the chest and lumbar region. Then I went to the clinic for a blood test. The doctor ordered a general blood profile with special emphasis on alkaline phosphatase enzyme profile.

The following Monday Dr. Newman would go over my latest blood test and X-ray reports of my chest and lumbar region. I felt a little nervous and my fear of the unknown made me nauseous. Ashley called me into the examination room, completed routine BP, pulse rate, temperature check-ups and recorded data on my medical chart then said, "The doctor will be here within a few minutes and left."

Dr. Newman came to my room greeted me as usual and then asked me how I was doing.

So far there was nothing unusual in Dr. Newman's behavior. Everything looked great and was a standard pattern I had experienced before from him. Then Dr. Newman told me that a bone in the lumbar region showed an arthritic and somewhat swollen area which needed further analysis including an MRI of the lumbar region. The alkaline phosphatase level was also very high which showed a phosphate imbalance. He referred me to see an orthopedic surgeon Dr. James Morris and requested me to see him as soon as possible.

I followed his order and arrived at Dr. Morris's office next day. Dr. James Morris showed me the MRI image of my lumbar region and said, "You have a tumor in your pelvis, and I suspect the tumor may be cancerous."

His words hit me like a thunderbolt and I felt nauseated. Dr. Morris calmly said, "Don't be too alarmed. I can easily remove the tumor from the pelvis." My mind went numb. I was no more me, I became an entity whose existence was slowly slipping away from my consciousness.

Dr. Morris recommended that we should do a biopsy of the tumor within two days to see if the tumor was aggressive or not.

A needle biopsy revealed that my tumor was a very aggressive type of chondro-sarcoma and needed to be excised as soon as possible. The test results read as, "Chondral sarcoma, grade G3 and stage IV B; metastasized to ribs and lungs."

Dr. Morris consulted Dr. Holmes, an oncologist to remove the tumor surgically by Thursday. The surgery went well and they removed a 3 cm wide mass of malignant tissue. I spent two days in the hospital and came back home. Every day when I come back home from my work or errands, my dog Gold waited for me sitting by the front door entrance. Once I was inside the house, she jumped up on me and barked while wagging her tail. But today no one came to greet me — the house was empty. Before going to the surgery, I left Gold at the pet sitter's house so that Kim would take care of her needs while I was away.

I sat on my sofa looking at the empty room and remembering my life. I was married once, but it did not last because my wife considered me a total failure compared to other men who were always busy driving their wives here and there, doing all the manly chores of the house, maintaining a beautiful lawn and organizing everything so that the house would look and feel like a home. I was a man who loved to sit on the sofa, watch hours of football games, and other sports. Deeply absorbed in the meaning of life, the philosophical merits of existence and analyzing why mankind created God to suit their own selfish interests was more my thing. Often, I wrote poetry and dreamed the impossible dreams. My activities were useless in the eyes of pragmatists. My wife was a realist. She did not believe in dreams that could not be achieved. In her life she achieved everything as far as education, wealth, and any tangible things necessary for a successful life.

Our life fell apart. She moved out and settled in a neighboring state, and I stayed in the same place because of my job. I worked in a Walmart as a supervisor and trained newly hired employees in the store as cashiers. I'd been working for Walmart for over twenty-five years and I was an easy-going, harmless person, happy with little things. A friend of mine who also worked at Walmart suggested I move to a fifty-five plus community, so I would have people of the same age group staying close by, so that the bite of loneliness could be less detrimental to my health. I'd been thinking about it. I realized that my carefree life was experiencing a series of challenges that steadily crumpled the scaffolding of my existence. My mind was attacked by an existential crisis that questioned the meaning of life, and the validity of my presence in this cosmos.

Two weeks went by. Chemotherapy and radiation treatment made me very weak, but I managed my life as best as possible. One of the main challenges was not the effects of chemo, but the daily habit of walking my dog. My hip hurt a lot because of pain. It travelled across my hip down to my toes and occasionally pulled the sciatic nerve that caused excruciating pain. All this pain forced me to lie down in the bed and forgo the habit of walking my dog.

In the morning when I wore my shoes Gold knew I would take her out for a walk. She danced with joy and her bright brown eyes twinkled like stars that exuded happiness and gratitude towards me. That look, emotion and feelings could soften the heart and soul of any person who was living. Now I was almost an invalid. My legs were stiff, and that forced me not take her out for a walk. She looked at me with sadness. I barely opened the back door of the house and let Gold stay inside the fenced backyard and run around as a free spirit.

Dr. Holmes the oncologist, told me the chemotherapy was not working, and the metastatic cancer cells were progressing quickly and spread out throughout my skeletal system. He suggested that I should leave my house and join an assisted living center where I could receive necessary day-to-day care as there were no family members around to help me.

That night I could not sleep. I was thinking about Gold, what to do with her. I had only two options left for the care of Gold. I could take her to a Humane Society where the agency could find a willing person to adopt a dog over thirteen years old, or put her to sleep by administering drugs. The first option to give her up for adoption was a humane way to take care of her needs as long as she was alive. People don't adopt very old dogs because their lifespan are short and they were not willing to spend their time, effort, money on a dog who would die in two years. The death of pets brings sadness and depression to their owners, so no one wants to adopt a very old dog. To find the right person for the situation would be difficult and perhaps impossible. The death of the original owner causes irreparable damage to a dog's health, and many die because they could not bear the separation anxiety.

The second option was to euthanize the dog so she would die with no pain and sufferings. Euthanasia was a good practice to help a suffering, critically ill pet to die peacefully. But to put a pet to sleep not because of poor health or suffering but because no one is there to take care of her/him? That is not right! Who decides? How to decide between existence versus reality OR living versus death?

Was there a God who can be the judge to decide? All these philosophical questions come from the power of human ethics and belief; can they conclude with absolute certainty?

After a long deliberation, I reached a decision that gave me some peace before my death, which was lurking. I gave Gold to the animal shelter so that the center would find a caring, loving person who would adopt Gold and receive a check of $1,000 for taking care of the dog. The shelter would receive $5,000 for finding a caring, loving dog owner who would adopt Gold with open arms, mind and heart.

I asked a neighbor to take me and Gold to the animal shelter. She jumped with joy and her bright eyes sparkled like stars. After arriving at the shelter, I put a leash on Gold and with a limp walked in the front courtyard. She was excitedly sniffing everything around the courtyard and wagging her tail with happiness. A short walk I could barely manage, defying the pain, to enjoy the last walk with Gold. Then I handed her to a shelter employee who took her away with him. As Gold was moving away, she barked twice. I started moving away from her with a limp. I did not look back at her. Distance between us extended further until I reached my neighbor's car. I heard some barking in the distance. Tears came down like a river — I felt at last I was free to die in peace!

NOORJAHAN

The Tilpi village next to Piyali River is a beautiful place to live. The village is surrounded in the west by a chain of hills rising 500 feet above the ground. Early morning when the sun rises the rays of sun are partly obstructed by the hills, but after some time the rays shine above the hills like a bright canopy and take away with it all the darkness of the night's sleeping veil. Various birds chirp loudly to conduct their cacophony. At times the symphony is broken by the loud, rough, and coarse noise emanating from the throats of crows — ka, ka, ka. A thin brook flows around the village where a large herd of cows are busy masticating grasses. A young man sits on the bank of the creek playing his flute. The dancing notes of the flute serenade the loneliness and solitude of life's existence.

Noor was very happy to move to Tilpi. She remembered her village in Noakhali which was just like Tilpi. She grew up in Noakhali where her father was a lawyer, went to school and finished class IX but could not finish high school because of the Hindu-Muslim riot. Muslims massacred Hindus as they were a minority in Noakhali. The brutality and savagery forced the family to leave Noakhali and move to Calcutta as refugees by train. She was only fifteen years old. The train was heading towards Calcutta but just before the border, Muslim gangs armed with daggers and guns stopped the train and dragged everybody out of the railroad cars and raped women and girls with unimaginable savagery. They killed many men and ran way with impunity when the military arrived on the scene. The military did not round up a single Muslim. This carnage, butchery and inhuman torture was leveled against innocent, unarmed Hindu men, women, girls, and children. Allah watched silently the screams, cries, sufferings, violence, and flowing blood. The military did not deter these savages. Even these gangs defied and defiled Allah by raising their bloody hands towards Mecca and screamed with delight to kill Kafirs. Allah did not stop their aggression. Was He there? Or killed by these hooligans?

Bullets killed Noor's father and brother. Her mother and grandmother were beaten severely and dumped in a ditch. The gangsters repeatedly raped Noor. Her bloody naked body was dumped also in the ditch. The military saved her, but her mother and grandmother were dead because of fractured head wounds. She survived the torture but became an abandoned child whose entire world crashed in front of her bleeding eyes!

Noor, along with many raped and battered women was placed in a refugee camp across the border. She lived there for six months before she joined a group of women going to Calcutta. They worked in the city garbage dumps and collected discarded newspapers, scrap metals, and broken glass jars from dawn to dusk. In the night some were forced to give their body to goondas and other perverted men in exchange for some rice or rootis and lentils to fill their empty stomach and survive for the next day. Many jumped in front of railway trains to end their wretched life. Even death refused to accept these living dead creatures and denied their freedom, so that death could enjoy their sufferings!

God, if He existed, left these people a long time ago. He

was tired of dealings with these subjects because these wretched people did not give Him what he wanted. God loved opulence and big temples filled with gold jewelry. He loved people who made golden statues of His likeness and showered him with rosewater and sandalwood scents. He loved big churches, cathedrals, mosques, and temples that were built to proclaim His mighty existence and greatness.

Noor used to pray regularly when she was small. Her experiences in life forced her to believe that there was no God. All religions emphasized that humans must suffer, because through sufferings they could prove to God their worthiness to be a part of God. These sufferings were necessary to purify the human soul and sanctify their existence. These teachings were the essence of all religious practices.

Noor asked herself the question, why God was not helping her to get away from this life? Why was He keeping her alive? This life was so miserable it was not at all worth living. She considered herself as living dead. God never answered her repeated prayers and requests. He simply stood in this giant void and watched silently the anguish, agony, sufferings, and torture. Noor felt that God was not yet satisfied with her sufferings. He wanted more from her. How much more suffering did she have to go through so that God would be happy and allow her to be a part of him? She pondered, but no answer came from heaven.

Meeting Mamtaz in the street and her motherly acceptance of Noor came from nowhere. Perhaps God opened a small door for Noor to pass through His abode and connected a bridge to Mamtaz. That connection was God's way of telling Noor that she had passed the test and became a part of God.

Mamtaz rented a house with four rooms in the basti close

to the bus station in Garia where many poor people lived. She opened a center called "Shanti Nivas" to entertain men in the night. She explained to Noor that she had to sell her body to men so she could earn some money. Half of the money she had to give to Mamtaz and the other half she could keep for herself. To keep herself alive, Noor became a besya. Mamtaz had two other young ladies working for her little bordello. She was fifty years old; no customer would come to her because she was too old for this profession. Three women including Noor supported Mamtaz and treated her with respect and love as their own mother.

Now she took the name of Noorjahan; her Hindu name was Arati, which her father gave her. After brutal rapes, goondas forced her to convert to Islam, and the Imam gave her a new name as Noorjahan. Hindu families did not accept Arati because she was raped and converted to Islam. Hindu Brahmins treated her as untouchable and outcast. The Muslims did not accept her because she was born and raised as a Hindu.

Hindu and Muslim men used to visit these women in the night to fulfill their carnal desire. Deep in the darkness sexual pleasure was enjoyed by these men, they did not care whether the woman was a Hindu or Muslim. At this moment the sexual pleasure erased all the religious taboos. The same group of men would swear that they disliked women of a different religion to cohabit with them. In the business of carnal pleasure, the religion, caste, creed, rich, poor and social outcasts were all same. They were here to enjoy the hellish orgasm!

In the same basti an artist and a budding writer rented a room in the complex where Mamtaz's little bordello was. In the center of the courtyard a tube well provided fresh water to all members of the community. The city provided only two water taps which operated in the morning between 6 and 8 am and in the evening between 6 and 9 pm. A long line used to gather around these water taps and people collected drinking water from them. The water quality from the tube well was not great for drinking but many used this water for drinking after boiling it. There were about six small wooden building with corrugated roofs made from asbestos. Each small building had three to four small rooms looking like elongated boxes. Mamtaz's building has a white signboard hanging in the house's front displaying the name "Shanti Nivas".

Police and members of local goondas often visited Mamtaz's "Shanti Nivas" for a restful night with no payment. She was a cunning Bordello operator, and by allowing police and goondas free visitation rights, she kept her business open with no disturbances and interruptions. Bribes complemented and protected the oldest profession of human pleasure alive and well for centuries.

Men and women used to take a bath using water from the tube well. Anand the artist would pull his chair from his room and sit there drawing women bathing. He used these women as his living models for developing his painting portfolio. His sketches of semi-naked women became alive in the multicolor portrait. He made a pictorial book of art of these women depicted in various bathing sequences. Women used only saris to cover their bodies during bathing. The wet sari would come off the body and expose their bosoms which made Anand draw with extraordinary passion and his fertile imagination raised these semi-naked women into a classic art of human existence with purity and innocence.

Anand was a commercial artist. He earned his living by working for an advertising agency. He created large posters for the advertising agency which were displayed along the roadside of highways. The day he was not working he would stay home and draw pictures of women taking a bath in the center of the courtyard.

Noor never bathed in the courtyard. She used to take a bath on her building veranda. She was shy about exposing herself in front of people. But in her profession shyness had no value, because exposure of body parts was the most attractive asset to lure her men. As Noor was very young her beauty attracted people, and they paid more money for her services. Mamtaz always protected Noor but at times, she would bargain with clients a higher price for Noor's services.

Anand drew all women who bathed regularly in the courtyard. He waited to catch Noor so he could draw Noor's body and metamorphose her into an angelic beauty filled with absolute innocence. One day Anand asked Noor if she would allow him to draw her portrait. Noor told him to ask Mamtaz if she would agree to this proposal. Mamtaz made a business deal with Anand and allowed him to draw her portrait but there'd be no nudity involved, only a pose where Noor would lie on a bed covered with a sari. Anand agreed to pay a sum of Rs.500 for this extraordinary opportunity.

Noor put on a yellow sari and a red dot on the forehead and painted her lips with red paint. She painted her eyelashes dark with *Kazol* that transformed her like an *Opsora*. It amazed Anand to see Noor's beauty and he drew a wonderful picture of her as if she were a divine *Opsora* coming down from heaven to greet her subjects.

Anand fell in love with Noor. He realized that in his lonely life, Noor could fill up his empty void. Noor also fell for Anand. One day Mamtaz had to go to her village Tilpi for business. Anand came to Noor's room and made love to her. This physical union was different because when two people are in love the physical union has a purity and meaningful connection beyond lust and desire. Only a union of a soul filled with happiness, ecstasy, and rapture. Noor felt that her life would change soon; she would have a man who was in love with her. She could build a new life where she would have human dignity and social acceptance. As a member of the social outcast because of her profession, Noor always felt that her life had no meaning. She always dreamt about love that was pure and would conquer all challenges and social injustice. At last, she could build a nest filled with happiness and leave this wretched life of prostitution.

Noor disclosed everything to Mamtaz. She said Anand asked her to be with him and leave this place and settle in Bombay where Anand was planning to move soon. In Bombay she could live in peace. Mamtaz grasped Noor's hand and said, "I am very happy to hear all these beautiful dreams but in life these dreams never come true. People say many good things without knowing how to achieve all these, because life is ruthless and filled with broken promises and frozen dreams."

Noor felt sad and disappointed to hear Mamtaz's negative implications, but she knew that Mamtaz was the only person who would do everything for Noor. She had proved already by saving Noor's life once when she was battered by vicious people, only Mamtaz had the courage to fight against these people and gave shelter to Noor so she could have a home.

Mamtaz took Noor as her own daughter and protected her from all evil.

Anand showered Noor with expensive saris, perfume and jewelries and told Mamtaz that Noor should not see other men because he would like to marry her. Anand offered Mamtaz Rs.1000 per month so that Noor would be with him in his little room next to Mamtaz's "Shanti Nivas." Mamtaz liked this business proposition and supported Anand's proposal. Mamtaz asked Noor what she thought about Anand's plan. Noor replied, "If you think this is good for us then I will follow your command."

Mamtaz felt blessed to know that Noor was in love with Anand. She had experienced love in her life for a brief period when her husband was alive. Through Noor's happiness Mamtaz experienced the lost beauty and enchantment of love in her mind and body that were deeply buried with Bismilla's tomb. She felt exhilaration because her daughter Noor was happy at last. Noor had suffered too much in her short life. Perhaps the time has come for Allah to pour His blessings on her. She closed her eyes and prayed for Noor's happiness and well-being.

Anand set a date for marrying Noor. He gave her a gold necklace with a star shaped blue stone in the center of the pendant during their engagement. Noor cried. Mamtaz was very happy for Anand to marry Noor. In one part of her heart she was overwhelmed with joy. At the same time, it filled with sadness, because of ensuing emptiness of Noor's absence in her life.

Anand received a new contract from an advertisement company from Bombay to paint large sign boards about movies along the national highway. He was getting ready to move to Bombay after the wedding. He was excited about his new job and married life with Noor and was counting the days for this new beginning in their life.

Anand was trying to finish his last assignment of painting a large billboard for an upcoming movie in Calcutta. The project involved hand-painted images of the hero and heroine on the canvas. He laid a huge canvas and almost finished the whole painting. He was a very meticulous artist. During work he became completely engrossed with his subjects so that each painted character became alive through each stroke of his paint brush.

The billboard was about eight feet long and five feet wide, fastened with the signpost which was twenty feet above the ground. The crew built a platform for the artist to stand and draw the pictures. Anand was busy painting the heroine's hair with his paintbrush on the canvas, when suddenly a car veered from the driving lane in the highway and slammed into the signpost which was a few feet away from the highway at high speed and burst into flame. The impact and the explosion caused Anand to lose his balance and fall onto the ground from the platform. He hit his head violently and blood splattered everywhere. He lost consciousness. The driver of the burning car was ejected from the car as he was not wearing a seat belt and landed in a ditch. Many people gathered at the scene and someone stopped a police jeep. The officer used his radio to contact the head office and requested an ambulance to take two people to the hospital. When an ambulance arrived carrying Anand and the car driver, doctors found both men had lost excessive blood and had deep fractures in their skull. They took them to the surgical unit and operated on them to stop internal bleeding and reduce neural hematoma. During surgery both men suffered cardiac arrest and died. Hospital doctors recorded the deaths of both men and a certificate posted time of death 5:15 pm.

Noor was busy cooking for Mamtaz and two other girls who worked for the evening. Sometimes Mamtaz asked Anand to join them for dinner. The girls had to finish their dinners and get ready for the evening welcoming and entertain the clients. The night spread its dark veil over the city. City lights with low wattage barely could remove the darkness that has spread. Noor placed an oil lamp made from clay on top her little dresser. She lit it with a matchstick and closed her eyes to pray Allah. This practice she followed every evening.

Noor waited for Anand to come home. Time passed by. Night became darker. Noor was restless. She knew that by 8 pm Anand came home every day. Somehow Noor could not focus on anything. She felt something was happening somewhere which would have a great impact in her life. Noor went to Mamtaz's room and sat with her. She said, "Mamtaz I am afraid of tonight. I feel tonight is trying to tell me something is terribly wrong." Mamtaz embraced her and said, "Don't worry; everything will be fine." The wall lizard made "tick, tick, tick," sound. These lizards were harmless creatures that lived in the house and kept the house free of insects.

Noor did not go to her room; she slept in Mamtaz's room that night. She was afraid of this dark night. Mamtaz always allowed Noor to come to her room and sleep with her whenever she wanted. Two girls who worked with Mamtaz knew her motherly affection towards Noor. They used to tease Noor and call her a baby. Noor just smiled at them saying nothing. She enjoyed this attention from Mamtaz and she adored her.

Noor could not sleep the whole night. She was awake, anxiously waiting to hear opening sound of Anand's door. But she heard nothing—only the cacophony of crickets filled the dark night!

In the morning around 10 o'clock a police jeep stopped in front of the basti. The police officer was looking for the quarters of Anand Siddique. A neighbor who knew Anand led the officer to Anand's quarter. The officer came to the door of the room and found it locked. He went to next quarter where the signboard read "Santi Nivas" and knocked at the door where Mamtaz lived. She opened the door, and the officer asked, "Do you know Anand Siddiqe?" Mamtaz knew something happened to Anand. Inside her mind she was nervous and petrified, but she kept a cool composure outside, and said, "I have known Mr. Anand as a neighbor for some time."

The officer asked her, "Do you know any close relatives of Mr. Siddique?

"No sir," Mamtaz replied.

"Can you give any information you might have regarding Mr. Siddique?"

"Mr. Siddique worked at Tillman advertisement agency as a commercial artist in Dalhousy Square," replied Mamtaz.

The officer asked, "Who owns this place?"

"Golan Mohammad owns this basti. We are renting these quarters," replied Mamtaz.

The officer left the place.

Noor overheard everything; she knew Anand is in trouble. But she was not sure what kind of trouble Anand was in. But her gut feeling told her Allah wanted her to suffer more.

100

Mamtaz held Noor in her bosom. Tears from both women rolled like river.

Anand did not return to his quarters…

Two days later in the afternoon a police car came to the basti. An officer and a police constable came to Anand's quarter, opened the door and combed through the room. They took away everything from the room and loaded it into a small police van and left the place. In the evening Golan Mohammad came to Mamtaz and asked about Anand. She told Golan that she knew Anand worked as a commercial artist and had a passion for drawing pictures of women. Some of her girls acted as models for him. She also mentioned that Anand was writing a book about women who suffered untold misery, torture, social abandonment and were outcasts with no reason.

Mamtaz asked Golan, "What happened to Anand?"

Golan kept silent for a few seconds. Mamtaz's heartbeat skipped beating for those few seconds of Golan's silence.

Golan said, "Mr. Siddique died in an accident."

"What kind of accident?"

"Mr. Siddique was painting the billboard when a car at high speed veered from the highway and flew into the billboard post and burst into flame. The impact caused Mr. Siddique to fall from the billboard platform to the ground 20 feet down below. He died two hours later in the hospital along with the driver of the car who crashed in the signpost," answered Golan.

It stunned Mamtaz to hear the news of Anand's death. She did not know how to tell Noor this tragic news. Noor would be devastated. She had suffered already horrendous experiences in her short life. How could she withstand more agony and anguish? Could Allah spare her from punishment to this young woman? Why was Allah testing her resilience and tormented soul?

Mamtaz suffered a lot in her young age. Her husband died when she was twenty-five years old. They had a fifty-acre tract of land in Tilpi and a large lake. Her husband Bismillah was a farmer. He grew vegetables and fruit trees on his land. He released baby Katla and Rohu fish in the lake which matured within three to six months, he then harvested them with a fish net and sold them in Calcutta markets. Bismillah made lot of money through these ventures.

During the Hindu-Muslim riot Mamtaz lost her husband. Hindu hooligans burned down their house. She with the help of some neighbors was able to rebuild her house. After Bismillah's death Mamtaz had to sell her body to get enough money to survive. She moved to Garia and rented a house with a corrugated roof in the basti around the bus stop. She became popular among the destitute ladies and developed a cooperative business of *"Bessya House."* Her business flourished because she knew how to control the police and local goondas. She would donate free services to people important in the society. She was known for her charm and brains.

Mamtaz's experiences, savviness and communication skills did not prepare her for how to break tragic news of Anand's death to Noor. But she had to tell this heartbreaking news to Noor. Mamtaz said to Noor, "Allah took away Anand from you and us."

Noor heard the dreaded news and fainted. Mamtaz placed Noor's head on her lap and placed a cold towel on her forehead. After a few minutes, Noor opened her eyes and said,

"Allah should have taken me with him. There is nothing left for me to live."

Mamtaz filled with melancholy whispered, "Never say there is nothing left for me. Allah designed this, so you can achieve something great in your life. He is testing you. He will give you peace and solace so you could overcome these tragic events in your life. I have had an experience the same situation when Allah snatched Bismillah from my embrace and left me in emptiness. I had to suffer so that I could rise up and keep living because that was Allah's design for me."

Noor answered in a whisper, "Allah does not care about me, and He is dead!"

"Hush! Do not desecrate Allah. He loves you. You are immature and you cannot see him. But He is there watching you."

Noor said nothing more.

Time passed by.

One day Noor visited the temple nearby. She was wearing a white sari with a red border, and a small red tip on her forehead showing a Hindu married woman. She went straight to the front of the Temple and sat near the idol of Ma Durga. The pujari was chanting in Sanskrit the great slokas of religious mantras. Noor focused her eyes on Ma Durga's eyes and tears rolled through her cheek. She could not hear slokas and the ringing of the bells. The incense and Arati with the fire all created an atmosphere that gave courage to Noor to ask Ma Durga a question, "Ma Durga, can you please tell me is there any meaning in my life and is it worth living?" Ma Durga did not reply to her question.

Noor realized that Ma Durga was not listening her prayers or her question. She got up, stood before the idol and

103

murmured, "Ma Durga, give me strength and will to continue my journey, until the day when I have to cover my flickering flame forever, so I will earn my freedom." She moved away from the idol, then suddenly, the pujari called her from behind, "Please take the holy blessings from Ma Durga."

She turned back and looked at the pujari who was holding the blessed Ganga Jal in his hand and placed a spoonful of holy water in her folded palms of the hand.

Noor looked at Ma Durga's eyes and felt *she* was smiling at her…

Noor tried to understand this experience in the Temple. She was convinced that Ma Durga answered her question and prayer via a telepathic code through her smile that validated her life's sufferings and agony. It convinced her that she would be free soon. Her wretched, tormented life was not in vain. It had meaning that her personal choices never failed her from any kind of wrongdoing. She was pure and a beautiful human being.

Noor told Mumtaz her whole experience in the Temple. Mumtaz hold her tightly and said, "Allah sanctified you. Now the time has come for you to visit the mosque." Noor happily accepted Mumtaz's suggestion. The following week Noor dressed up with Salwar and Kameez and headed for the mosque. All women sat on one side and men sat on the other side of the mosque. The imam was standing on the minbar — a raised platform from which he addressed his congregation. That day the imam was telling a story about the prophet Mohammad and how he explained Allah's power and justice.

Noor looked at the imam who was standing in front of the minbar and continued his sermon. The imam said, "One day, a man brought his son with him to the mosque and asked the prophet Mohammad, my son likes to eat molasses and sweetmeat whenever he can get some. To satisfy his desire to eat molasses, he would steal it from the kitchen even though his mother forbade him. 'Oh, Prophet of Allah, please tell my son not to eat molasses anymore? My son will obey your directive, because he believes in you'."

Mohammad looked at the man and said, "Please come next week to the mosque with your son and I will talk to your son about this issue."

It disappointed the man that the prophet did not fix the problem right away, but he realized that Mohammad had so many problems to solve for mankind, he needed more time. "So," he said, "Prophet Mohammad, I will bring my son next week".

The following week the man and his son arrived at the mosque. They entered the center of the hall where the prophet Mohammad was sitting on a carpet. Mohammad greeted them and asked the boy, "Why do you like to eat molasses even though your mother told you not to eat it?"

"I love the sweetness on my tongue when I slurp the molasses. It makes me happy," the boy replied.

The prophet looked at the boy and said, "It makes you happy but when your mother told you something you must not do then you must follow her wishes, because your parents love you and take care of you, so you can grow and flourish in life and be somebody Allah created you to become. Instant happiness sometimes may be bad for your well-being which you might not be able to see in that particular moment of happiness. Parents are your protectors, supporters, and everything in your life so you can grow up and lead a healthy, prosperous, happy, meaningful life. Eating molasses in excess can take away your life's happiness by creating diseases."

The boy was happy to hear the prophet's simple sermon and said, "I will not steal molasses again. If my mother gives me some to eat, only then I will eat it."

Mohammad smiled at the boy and touched his head. The father was thrilled that his son promised not to steal and obey his parents' wishes. But he could not understand why the prophet asked him to wait a week to hear his decision. Curiosity was disturbing his mind so he asked the prophet, "Why did we have to wait a week to hear your answer?"

Prophet replied, "I told you to come next week because I had to practice what I preach."

It baffled the man and he looked at Mohammad with a blank expression and said, "Oh Prophet of Allah could you explain what you meant?"

Mohammad smiled and said, "I love molasses and I ate a lot whenever I could get hold of it. So, I had to stop eating molasses before I could ask your son not to eat it."

The man understood why the prophet had asked him to come next week.

Noor heard the sermon from the imam and learned the wisdom from Mohammad that in life whatever you do you must be truthful to yourself and your actions.

After the sermon Noor focused her attention on the Qiblah wall particularly in the center where a depression or Mihrab could be seen. This depression represented the direction of Mecca. She prayed to Allah to give her wisdom that would help her face the challenges of life. She closed her eyes and asked, "Prophet Mohammad please tell me is there any meaning in my life that warrants living?" The semicircular depression on Mihrab created a feeling of vertigo in Noor's head. She felt the whole room was spinning like a top, and she was floating in empty space. She could not keep her head erect; she fell on the floor of the prayer hall...

When she opened her eyes, she found her head resting on the lap of an older woman who was gently pressing a wet cold towel on her forehead. The old woman smiled at her and said, "You are safe and take a rest. Allah is with you."

Noor asked, "Where am I? Who are you?"

The woman replied, "You are in the mosque and I am the wife of the imam and my name is Fatima."

Noor experienced a serene feeling. She felt the touch of her deceased mother. Noor remembered that when she was very young her mother would place her head on the lap and gently run her delicate fingers through her long, curly hair. After a few hours of rest Noor felt well and Fatima volunteered to take her to Mamtaz's place.

In the evening, Fatima and her husband fetched a rickshaw and took Noor to her house. Fatima told Mamtaz how Noor fainted in the mosque. She also suggested that Noor needed to see a doctor because her sudden sickness might be because of pregnancy. Noor was very surprised to hear Fatima's suggestion she might be pregnant. Noor and Mamtaz both showed gratitude to Fatima and the imam and thanked them for their hospitality and care.

Mamtaz told Noor to rest for few days and avoid customers until she felt better. She recognized if Noor was pregnant then she had to leave this place and go back to an interior village in Tilpi where Mamtaz owned a thatched house. Noor could raise her child peacefully there.

Mamtaz could not bear a child but always wanted to have one. She felt the prophet Mohammad asked Gabrielle to bring this child to Noor so she could adopt this child and raise her/him. Maybe it was Allah who was fulfilling Mamtaz's desire via Noor's pregnancy. It was indeed a blessing from God that she would receive soon.

Noor could not sleep that night. She realized if she was pregnant then she had to leave this place and go back to the street where people would abuse her, beat her, call names and other nonhuman treatment, just because she was a homeless woman.

Mamtaz treated Noor like her own daughter. But in a brothel a pregnant woman had no place to live. So, she had no choice but to tell Noor to leave this place and go somewhere else. Noor thought about her options are in this situation.

She had only three options such as aborting the baby or living in the street and undergoing brutality and rape every day or committing suicide by jumping in front of the coming train. She could not decide what option would be best for her so she asked Hindu Goddess Ma Kali, Muslim Allah, and Christian Jesus for help. But she received no help from anyone. She was very depressed and felt that no one cared about her plight, no one was there to help, and perhaps gods from all religions were disgusted with her and wanted her to go to hell because of her sins.

Noor was impure and abandoned by everybody even the Almighty. She was helpless and cried a whole night for her miserable life. In her short life Noor had experienced brutality, rape, brushed with death quite a few times, but by unforeseen force somehow was saved from death. She never complained to anyone about her wretched condition, only asked a question to God about what the meaning of her life is and why she existed.

The next day Mamtaz took Noor to a clinic for the poor for a checkup. The doctors checked her and did some blood and urine tests and told them to come back a week later for the results of the tests. Mamtaz and Noor both felt that time was not moving fast enough. They anxiously awaited the results. Mamtaz was praying to Allah that the test result would reveal Noor was pregnant so she will get her wishes fulfilled to own a child. Noor asked God not to give her a child because having a child would destroy her life and erase her from this existence!

It was Friday. Mamtaz and Noor arrived at the clinic at around nine o'clock in the morning. They had to wait another hour before they were called in by the nurse and entered the examination room. The doctor came to the room and said, "Congratulation Noorjahan, you will be a mother soon."

A thunderbolt flashed outside as if it wanted to take away Noor's soul with it. But Noor was composed, a slight smile came to her lips, and she uttered, "All is Allah's wish."

Mamtaz hugged Noor tightly and said, "Yes, it is Allah's wish."

Tears came gushing from Mamtaz's eyes, as if the flood gate of unfulfilled desire came out of bondage and liberated itself into the vastness of a living life.

Mamtaz told Noor she had a small house in a village of Tilpi fifty miles away from Garia. Most of the inhabitants were poor sharecroppers who grew rice and seasonal vegetables. Noor should leave Garia and stay there with Mamtaz. She would ask

Latifah to run her business. Noor could join the village school teaching small children the rudiments of reading, writing, and arithmetic as she attended high school before forced to join the bordello.

Noor and Mamtaz left Garia and went to the village where Mamtaz had a small thatched house. Noor after a long time could sit quietly in a place where she could contemplate and reflect on her past life that was filled with torture, brutality, and fear of death. She was happy that Mamtaz became her mother, and the developing baby in her womb would make her a mother soon. That innate desire to survive and procreate was strong enough to erase the pain and sufferings of life and did not hinder her self-worth and self-realization. She never compromised her moral value, because motherhood was more sacred and purer than the social approval of a moral code imposed by the society. The society and religion abandoned her just because Muslims raped her, the Hindus left her naked among men who devoured her physically, mentally, and spiritually but were not willing to render a helping hand to save her.

The Muslims were responsible for human brutality and bestiality, but Mamtaz — a Muslim herself was strong enough to defy that violence-filled, blood thirsty atmosphere and save Noor from death.

Mamtaz was kind enough to take Noor in her bosom and gave her an opportunity to live with her. Even though Mamtaz was a prostitute, and society treated her as a social pariah, and outcast she had a far superior understanding of humanity filled with love, affection and care. Morality should be intertwined with love, affection and understanding so not only the social code but the circumstances that forced an individual to deviate from the social guideline could judge it. In extraordinary circumstances we can forsake social order or code. This flexibility enriches the social order and makes it more humane.

Religions controlled by religious zealots stretch their religion's control to a point where the normal flexibility of religious values are so narrowly interpreted that it becomes a noose to the people who are liberal and more open to compromise. They are the first victims of the religion's constraint and fall out of the religion and become a non-practicing religious group. Sufferings and challenges are part of existence. If you exist, you must suffer. But why? Many philosophers proposed that sufferings are the purification process of God, which when achieved then the individual arrives to a new state where they become a part of God itself. To justify the existence of God, struggle and sufferings become the tool of a purification process.

Mamtaz and Noor settled in Tilpi. Noor's pregnancy progressed with no complication and she gave birth to a baby boy. Mamtaz was thrilled to hold a child in her hands which she longed for many years. At last Allah heard her prayer and gave her the greatest gift a woman could have. She was euphoric and told Noor, "This boy is mine. You can have many more if you wish but this one you have to give me. My dry breast cannot feed the baby so you have to feed him for me. This is my only request I have from you."

Noor said, "Mamtaz you are my mother, and you took me in your bosom as your child. Both of us will raise this baby together."

Mamtaz cried with happiness. Both women shared their joyous expectation of motherhood together. Mamtaz named the baby boy Mohamed.

Noor started her new job in the village kindergarten school as a teacher. She taught children the rudiments of writing and reading Bengali alphabets, arithmetic and visual expression of various fruits, vegetables, fishes, and domesticated animals.

Ten years went by. Now Mohamed was ten years old. He was fond of learning and loved to read books. Noor pushed her son to study hard and Mohamed followed his mother's wishes as if Allah had directed him. Mohamed passed class six with flying colors and stood first in the class. The school district selected him as their candidate for a full scholarship to study at Garia Residential High School. Mohamed moved to the city and started his education at the school. In the beginning Mohamed missed his mother and Mamtaz, but both insisted that he should stay there and focus on his educational experiences so he could excel in everything that was required of him.

One day when Noor was in the school, Mamtaz felt a severe pain in her chest, and passed out in the verandah in her house. The next-door neighbor found her lying on the veranda, and blood trickled from her nostrils. A group of women gathered around Mamtaz and notified Noor to come home and tend to Mamtaz. Noor rushed to the local dispensary to fetch the doctor and brought him with her in a rickshaw. The doctor examined her and advised Noor to take Mamtaz to the hospital a few miles away. When Mamtaz arrived at the hospital her weak heart stopped pumping blood to her body. Noor collapsed in the hospital after hearing the doctor's verdict that Mamtaz was dead. Death took her away with him and gave her eternal peace and ultimate freedom she was longing for a long time.

When Noor recovered her senses, she felt a dark veil of melancholy covered her mind, spirit, and senses. For the second time in her life she experienced the dread and anguish filled with a sense of abandonment by Allah. She asked, "Allah how much suffering do I have to go through so you would give your blessings to me and liberate me from this earth, so I could achieve my freedom?"

No answer came from Allah, only silence carried a sigh with him in the void.

Noor sent a telegram to Mohamed to come home and bury Mamtaz as the men only can carry the last rites of the deceased loved ones. Mohamed was only fourteen years old. Mohamed hugged the cold lifeless body of Mamtaz, cried loudly and said, "Amma, why did you leave us so soon? Who will look after Ma?" No answer came from Mamtaz. Only the sound of sobbing filled the room.

The death of Mamtaz made Noor very lonely and created a giant void in her day-to-day existence. Mamtaz was more than Noor's mother. She occupied every facet of her life. Noor did not know how to cope with this void. Mohamed was away studying in the residential school and Noor felt she had to hold on to something that would help her overcome this loneliness. She chose the village school as a refuge and put all her energy and mind in the school.

Time slowly passed by. Mohamed finished high school as an outstanding student and received a scholarship to attend Presidency College in Calcutta, which was one of the best colleges in India. He majored in Physics Honors. Noor felt Allah accepted all her sufferings, bestowed real happiness and the meaning of life to her. Noor's father was a lawyer, and he had studied at Presidency College. Now her son and deceased father both would have an invisible bond that was destined to happen by the blessings of Allah.

Mohamed received his bachelor's degree in applied physics with a first-class honor ranking, from the Presidency College when he was only twenty years old. By the age of twenty-two, he earned a Master's of Science degree with a first-class and ranked third in the University. He impressed his physics professors with his intellectual ability and maturity as a scholar, so they recommended him to Duke University in America. Duke University offered him a research fellowship that covered all expenses including room, board, tuition, and living expenses worth more than $25,000 a year.

Noor was thrilled for Mohamed's achievement in academia and his development into a nice, gentle man with exceptional abilities and qualities. She always thanked Allah for his blessings and developed a blind, unquestionable trust towards the existence of Allah.

Once Mohamed settled into his doctoral studies in the States, he brought his mother to America so that Noor would not feel lonely anymore. In the summer recess Mohamed flew to Calcutta and escorted his mother to board a Boeing 747 jumbo jet. Noor had never flown in her life before, so she was scared to board the plane. She was very happy that her son was taking her in America but felt she was leaving Tilpia, the village where she had spent most of her life, and experienced loving embrace of Mamtaz, the smiles of school children and beautiful memories that kept her alive.

She had to leave everything behind. Past led to present. Life's journey started with horrible, torturous experiences she had to bear and fought valiantly to overcome those challenges and kept on moving forward, so that a better day would come someday. Her belief and resolute tenacity regarding life's existence complemented by the presence of Allah's blessings made Noor feel that life after all had some special meanings. Before she was not sure why she should live.

Mohamed asked his mother to take the window seat, so she could see the floating clouds and a glorious sunset that turned a majestic display of bright red on the horizon. The plane was getting ready to take off, waiting for the clearance from the control tower. Once the Captain received clearance, the aircraft moved very fast on the runway for takeoff. Noor closed her eyes in fear. Mohamed held his mother's hand tightly with absolute assurance. The airplane lifted off the ground effortlessly like a giant bird. Mohamed told Noor, "Ma, you can open your eyes now."

Noor opened her eyes and saw the giant plane gliding in the air as a free bird.

The aircraft approached New York airport. Mohamed pointed out the Statue of Liberty to his mother and said, "You are in the land of free."

Noor was speechless as she saw the bustling city filled with many skyscrapers, thousands of people and cars moving here and there giving a false impression of chaos, but in reality, following a strict order! Mohamed showed his mother a slice of New York life, then took the Greyhound bus to go to Durham, North Carolina the home of Duke University. Mohamed rented a one-bedroom house close to the university. Noor was happy to see her son matured into a caring, intelligent adult. There were many resemblances between Anand and Mohammad. Anand was a caring, dreamy eyed man whose love and affection mesmerized Noor, and won her heart, but Allah took him away from her without giving her a chance to experience the blissful life filled with dreams. Her unfulfilled dreams dragged her into misery and sufferings again. Noor lost all hope. Allah took Anand away but left Mohamed in Noor's body to nurture, nourish, and raise him to become a man.

Mohamed took his mother to a neighbor's house where another Indian family lived. Joya and Prakash Ghose lived with their son Mridul who was a doctoral student at Duke University in biotechnology. Joya and Noor became close friends.

A group of Duke University students from India, Bangladesh, and Burma (now Myanmar), formed an organization known as "Freedom for Rohingya (FOR)" in the city. This organization educated and developed an awareness to the American public the plight of the Rohingya people, so that Americans could support Rohingya's plea for freedom from Burmese atrocities and torture. American policy towards Rohingya genocide was non-existing. If America took a strong stand against human carnage and genocidal rape in Rohingya, then the United Nations and other countries would condemn the Burmese Government's inaction policies and force the military to stop indiscriminate rape and violence against women and girls that resulted in a massive refugee crisis in Bangladesh.

Mohamed became a member of Freedom for Rohingya organization and took part actively in the cause of Rohingya because he heard a lot of stories about religious riots between

Hindus and Muslims during the partition of India and the Bangladesh liberation war. Noor disclosed her personal sufferings and murder of her whole family by the Muslim religious zealots. Mohamed knew Noor was born into a Hindu family but because the Muslim hooligans raped her Hindu families rejected her; only Mamtaz accepted her as her own daughter. This noble and loving gesture convinced Noor to follow Islam which absorbed her in their society. Mamtaz once described to Mohamed how purity and innocence of religion had been hijacked by the religious leaders to gain power so they could control their religion to use it the way they would like. This abuse of power transformed religions as one of the most vicious instruments to divide people and sow the seeds of hatred and lust for blood. The result was visible all over the world for centuries.

Mamtaz had advised Mohamed that all religions were pure and good. All gods/prophets were the same. All were part of our humanity. Love, care, acceptance, and noble duty to serve others were the tenets of all religions. Always believe in yourself and do your best whatever you are doing. Mamtaz's wisdom guided Mohamed's life. He believed in Mamtaz and followed the path of righteousness. The Rohingya's sufferings attracted his attention because he realized that he should help in whatever way so that justice would be done to these people.

A few months before, Mohamed gave an emotional speech in front of a large crowd gathered to hear the plights of Rohingya people in the student union building. People from the city, university and neighboring colleges came to protest the refusal of Burmese government to punish its military leaders for the recent brutal repression of innocent Rohingya people in the Rekhine state.

In that gathering Mohammad said, "President Suu Kyi refused to curb the genocide of Rohingya people even though they are a part of Burmese Federation for centuries. She has not yet exerted her authority to stop atrocities committed by her military and Buddhist mobs. When Suu Kyi did not have the power, she fought for all the people of Burma to remove military rule in Burma and establish democracy, but when she became the head of Burma, she had not yet exerted her authority to stop genocidal rape against women and girls of Rohingya people. Suu Kyi has not yet supported the birthright of Rohingya people as the bona fide Burmese, but she believes that Rohingya people belong to Bangladesh and they must go back and leave Burma. This distortion of the history of Rohingya people has caused tremendous human misery to these people."

The United Nations gave lukewarm support for the Rohingya people. They belonged to the Burmese Federation but had not yet supported the idea that Rohingya people should have their own independent state.

"The Rohingya people are part and parcel of Burma. Their sovereign rights as a citizen of Burma must be accepted and honored because they have been a part of Burma for centuries. We must preserve the minority status. Nobody should violate their birthright as Burmese. Their existence is in the soul of Burmese existence. By denying Rohingya's existence they are hurting or refusing Burmese existence.

"The political force energized by the fanatic Buddhist religious zealots cannot and should not impose the elimination of Rohingya people by genocide and/or other instruments of death and torture. We must stop this oppression. The world order must prevent these human sufferings. The humanity must prevail so that human race could survive. If we cannot stop this murderous lust for blood, then the survival of human race is in jeopardy.

"Please write letters to your respective Congressmen and Senators of your district and the state so they will give their support for the freedom of Rohingya people and push the President and the United States of America to support the plights of Rohingya people. America must support the rights of Rohingya people and legitimacy of their existence as a part of Burma, and not as refugees in Bangladesh.

"I call on all people, all religious faith, shades of color and various towns to join into a single call, a single voice of unity, and a deep belief that all people belong to the same human race, and pursue the truth for human freedom. Let Rohingya live in peace and prosper among all Burmese Federation with full dignity and honor. Long live Rohingya!"

A college student named Angkasa San, a Buddhist from Rangoon (Yangon), Myanmar (Burma) was moved by the passionate speech of Mohamed came to thank him and said, "I am very sad to know the plight of the Rohingya people caused by our military and Buddhist religious zealots. The military prevented journalists from reporting atrocities caused by the military on the Rohingya. The military jailed many newspaper journalists who dared to discuss the plights of Rohingya people. People of Burma do not know the extent of brutality and tortures caused by Buddhists on Muslim minorities. I am ashamed that I belong to the Buddhist majority. Please accept my sincere apology and I promise to do everything to support the cause of the Rohingya people."

The sincerity of this young woman surprised Mohamed and felt proud that he had the power to deliver an eloquent speech that could influence a person's opinion and thought process. Mohamed thanked her and said, "Please join our meeting again next month at the University of North Carolina, Chapel Hill."

The Freedom for Rohingya (FOR) movement spread fast among college and university students across America. The delegation from FOR organization was received well at the United Nations and the United Nations pushed the world opinion to stop carnage in Burma. Suu Kyi's administration agreed to stop the military actions against the Rohingya people and allow them to resettle in Rakhine state, Anakan Province. The American government played a leading role in influencing the United Nations Security Council.

Freedom for Rohingya has yet to achieve this but some progress towards the main goal has been established and stopped the brutality and genocidal rape of women and girls. Some perpetrators of this genocide have been punished and jailed.

Once the Freedom for Rohingya movement took center stage in colleges and universities, and received the backing of American politicians, Mohamed focused on his research project so he could finish a doctorate degree program in biophysics. He submerged himself in finding out the secrets of small interfering RNA (SiRNA) that could block cancerous growth in humans.

Previous research showed that SiRNAs have very short *in vivo* half-life and can be broken down by nucleases, which makes SiRNA unsuitable for therapeutic uses. To protect its SiRNA from degradation, Mohamed along with other groups suggested using biological cages (liposomes). He used gold nanoparticles coated with Polyethylene imine (PEI) which binds with negatively charged SiRNA. This gold nanoparticle-SiRNA-PEI complex when injected into a mice tumor site showed extensive apoptotic response and shrinkage of tumor tissues with no significant negative side effects[1].

Mohamed and his group also used gold Nano particles coated SiRNA-PEI complex on human cancer cell cultures, showed extensive cell death and suppression of cellular proliferation suggesting Gold Nano particle-SiRNA complex can be used to control tumor progression and a strong candidate for human clinical trials.

Mohamed's research professor approved his work and asked him to submit it to the dissertation committee. The committee also approved his work for a doctorate degree in biophysics. Besides earning a doctorate degree, Mohamed received a prestigious NIH post-doctoral fellowship award at Bethesda, Maryland. On the day of commencement, Mohamed took Noor and Angkasa to the graduation ceremony. Noor watched with pride and joy as her son achieved one of the most important recognitions in academia.

Five years after earning his doctorate degree and post-doctoral studies, Mohamed received a faculty position at a private university in North Carolina. Mohamed asked Angkasa to marry him and she accepted his proposal. Angkasa asked Noor for her blessing and she with great joy embraced Angkasa and said, "I know you are the most beautiful woman in the world, and Mohamed is the luckiest man to have you as his wife. May Allah protect and bless you both." Tears of joy

---

[1] Ozcan, G., Ozpolat, B., Coleman, R.L., Sood, A.K., and Lopez-Berestein, G. (2015). Preclinical and clinical development of SiRNA-based therapeutics. Adv.Drug.Deliv.Rev. 87, 108-119.]

and happiness merged between two women into a stream that nourished the thirsty ground and sowed the seeds of new dreams.

Angkasa tapped Mohamed to wake up because she felt a strong contraction in her belly. Mohamed had already prepared the suitcase filled with necessary clothing for Angkasa to wear in the maternity room. Besides her clothing, Mohamed packed a pink dress and a tunic pant for the newborn baby to wear. Noor was up from her bed; she was waiting for the day when her first grandchild would greet her.

Contractions became stronger with periodic intervals. Mohamed took Angkasa and Noor in his car and drove fast to the emergency room at the nearest hospital.

The hospital staff put Angkasa on the gurney and rushed her to the delivery room. Mohamed and Noor sat in the waiting room. Five hours have gone by with no news from the delivery room, it worried Mohamed, and he was pacing restlessly in the waiting room. Noor was calm and composed because she knew some women went through labor pains for a long period. Then at six o'clock in the morning a nurse came by the waiting room and asked Mohamed and Noor to follow her.

The nurse asked Mohamed to enter the maternity ward which was enclosed in a glass paneled rectangular shaped room where six beds lay side-by-side. There was enough room between each bed for a cubicle that separated other beds by sliding soft vinyl curtains to maintain privacy. The nurse led Mohamed to a cubicle where Angkasa was lying on the bed. A baby boy was resting on her bosom peacefully. Mohamed looked at Angkasa with a radiant, sweet smile, and said, "Allah gave us a wonderful gift that will make us very thrilled and contented throughout our lives." He held his wife's hand and kissed her lips. The boy was sleeping, ignoring the presence of his father!

The nurse brought Noor with her to see the baby. Tears of joy flooded Noor's cheeks. She held Angkasa's hand and whispered, "I want to name him Akbar. He is truly a part of Allah."

Angkasa said, "Ma, this baby is yours. We will name him Akbar as you wanted. Without your sacrifice and love we would never be able to see this beautiful child. It is a miracle and the will of God bestowed on us."

The next day Angkasa and the baby came home from the hospital. Noor lifted the baby and rested him on her chest, then pulled her nipple out, gently placing it on the lips of Akbar. The baby suckled the nipple, but no milk came out. Noor said, "My breasts are dry. They have lost their value. Angkasa you have to feed him for me."

Angkasa replied, "Ma, you raised Mohamed with your love, nourished him with your milk, and nurtured him with everything you had that made him what he is today. I ask you to bless me so I could give Akbar everything I have and make him a man with great qualities and characters just like Mohamed."

Noor remembered the day when Mamtaz brought her and the baby from the hospital and said, "Noor I want the baby." Then she placed her nipple on the baby's mouth. The baby suckled the breast, but no milk came out. Mamtaz said, "Dry breasts are useless. Noor you have to feed the baby so I can enjoy the motherhood Allah denied me. Through you I can fulfill my womanhood to be a mother — the ultimate desire of all women in the world."

Today Noor has completed the circle of life. The instinct of motherhood is so powerful and invigorating that it can accept, surpass, and overcome the challenges of life that filled with torture, rape, humiliation, poverty, and outcast. Human existence complemented with the motherhood of a woman makes the life worth living and saved the human species that shows the glorious spirit of humanity and human ingenuity. Resilience and belief in the human spirit live in the women like Mamtaz/Noor. They are in the front row leading the march towards the beauty of life and revealing the meaning and essence of life to all followers. Their sacrifice, sufferings, courage, and determination are the envy of God, and perhaps, they might be the true force that mirrored the human existence!

LAUGHTER YOGA

Sunshine Adult Care facility in Florida is a place where many patients who needs palliative care live and call their home. Patients who live there want a place where they can receive adequate medical care and a place to mingle with people in a similar situation as a closely knit community with dignity and respect.

Most of the clients who live in this facility know that they are waiting for death to appear at any minute. They have come to the end of their journey of life and they are like a flickering flame dancing around gasping for air before it shuts down its flame and erases their existence. Many members of this community undergo depression and existential sufferings, where they experience the feelings of dread, powerlessness, and a sense of loss of control of their living entity.

Death prowls stealthily around the facility with a great interest on each patient's affairs as if it is a caring person who wants to ameliorate pain and sufferings of these individuals. With all this gloom and suffering, the caregivers are always ready and willing to bring happiness and joy to these patients by entertaining them with various activities like singing, dancing, comic, magic shows, and laughter yoga.

Laughter is a beneficial activity for all people, particularly people with terminal illness. The process of laughter allows an extra load of oxygen to the lungs which facilitates higher energy levels and enhances the immune system, lowers blood pressure, and increases the production of endorphins which makes people happy. All these positive physiological activities boost the human mind, body and spirit and reduces the effects of depression and gloom.

Before starting laughter yoga all participants warm up by doing a breathing exercise. Everybody takes a long deep breath in and exhales air through their nostril. After repeating inhale and exhale of air ten times the participants start the yoga exercise. Laughter yoga exercises the lungs by making a loud noise of HO-HO, HE-HE, and HEY-HEY with a burst of high-pitched shrieks. These exhalations of shrieks release a high volume of air from lungs which starts and stimulates a high intake of oxygen to the lungs that energizes a person's body.

Friday afternoons are very special to these old people because the program of the laughter society will bring comedians to entertain the members of this community. After the comic show all participants gather in the central hall of the facility and join in the laughter yoga exercise.

The laughter yoga class was one of the most popular activities for the members because the meaningless sound of HO-HO, HE-HE, and HEY-HEY reminds them of their childhood. During early childhood children make meaningless noise and laugh for no reason. The silly noise and bright laughter from the children made their parents happy and proud that their child is contented. These memories brighten these old people and they can go back and reflect those precious and magical moments etched in their minds.

It was a Friday afternoon. The laughter yoga class started

as all clients were excited to take part. This exercise boosts their desire to live for another day, a moment or second. Patients with dementia sometimes remember their forgotten past, which brightens their life and boosts their desire to live fully for another day. Depressed souls who remember only the failures of their lives and find fault with everyone around them sometimes forget the depressed entity burdened with the thought of negativity, light up their mind through laughter yoga. High-pitched HO-HO sound forced them to practice something new, silly, and perhaps a childlike exuberance of air gushing out of their lungs that rejuvenate and excite their thought full of vigor.

The laughter session was in full swing. Screaming sounds of HO-HO, HE-HE, and HEY-HEY filled the room with energy, enthusiasm, and happiness. Everybody smiled with everybody like children who giggle for no reason, no reward, or expression, but only the innocence of their living entity.

Martha, a regular member of the laughter society felt a sharp pain in her chest and a shrieking noise gushed out of her chest. That noise differed from the shrieking noise of others. That noise was so different from other similar sounds that everybody noticed something else was happening here. All sounds stopped and everybody became silent. The shrieking painful noise hijacked the sound of laughter bursting out of Martha's chest. That haunting sound pierced the silence of the room another time and Martha collapsed on her chair.

Martha had never experienced this excruciating pain before. She realized that her life had come to an end. Then she felt she was floating in air like a feather. Her weightless body could swing and could bend her body like a fish defying her arthritic pain she suffered all her life. She was free; she felt a serene, soothing existence she had never experienced before. She started to climb up in an empty space, where she saw an arch of a gate standing before her. This mighty gate hung in space where time stood still.

A silhouette of a person appeared before her, who was standing guard in front of the arched gate. Martha tried to pass through the gate. The silhouette transformed into a man with a long beard that covered almost every part of him. The man signaled her to stop. She stopped. From the bottom of silence, a sound whispered, "This is the tunnel of Hell. Pass through three tunnels—the tunnel of Hell, the tunnel of Heaven, and the tunnel of Death. Once you have completed your visit to these tunnels, decide where you would like to live."

Tunnel of Hell: People who committed torture, mayhem, war, abuse, jealousy, criminal activity that lead to human misery and sufferings will be punished and live in this space of sufferings.

The tunnel of Hell looked like a maze. Martha started her journey through this maze with some apprehension and fear. She heard many horrible things present in the Hell. She was nervous and hoped that she would not experience any kind of dismemberment of her body or someone else's body. As she approached, she saw a human form and was afraid to look at the person's face, but the person stopped her and asked, "Why are you avoiding looking at me?"

Martha said, "I am fearful to look at you because I do not want to face a person who is condemned into Hell."

The person flashed a smile filled with snakes, and said, "Hell is my home because I was abusing people around me. For this reason, I am in the Hell, so I could repent for my sinful acts I imposed on other people."

Martha looked at the man and noticed that snakes turned into a blob of fireball inside his mouth.

A cold shiver bathed Martha's body and mind. But she did not lose her composure because she knew that she abused nobody in her life. She moved a little faster to see what was ahead of her path. She noticed another tunnel standing in front of her passageway.

This tunnel marked the tunnel of Death. She proceeded towards the tunnel of Death and found no one was there. An empty space was filled with a void. She realized that when life reaches its final destination everything stops in its track. The depth of the void engulfs the existence of a person's presence from the day he/she was born to the end of his/her journey — only a memory lingers in the void that the person existed as a living being but no longer has the liberty to exist. Everything stops.

Martha felt no gloom as she was exposed to the void and was not yet ready to consummate her desire to die.

Martha moved along the void for some time. The vastness made her cling with the innate desire to prolong her self-survival and gave her extraordinary strength to cope with loneliness and hopelessness. She survived the deep void and arrived at the third tunnel.

This was the tunnel of Heaven. This was a place where life was abundant, peaceful, filled with joy and happiness, where love bloomed into a vibrant, colorful spring and filled the air with the charming laughter of children and innocence that radiated like the soft sunshine in a rainbow.

Martha did not stop in the tunnel of Heaven; instead she marched forward to the end of the circular space where the arch of the gate could be seen. She tried to step out of the gate but an unforeseen energy held her in the empty space. Suddenly, Martha saw the silhouette of the person with a great beard appear before her and he commanded, "You have seen and passed through all three tunnels, now you must decide where you would like to live?"

Martha replied, "I have seen all three tunnels but you have not shown me the place where I really wanted to live."

The man asked her, "How come? I have shown you all the places that exist in this cosmos."

Martha replied, "No, you have not shown me all the choices that exist in the infinitum."

It baffled the man to hear her answer. He looked at Martha with his piercing eyes, and asked her, "Where do you want to live?"

Martha replied, "I want to live in a separate space which I call the tunnel of existence."

The old man flashed a smile at Martha and disappeared.

The wailing sound of the ambulance pierced the air. The ambulance car number 101 carrying Martha delivered her in the emergency room of the hospital. The attending nurse screamed "code blue". Doctors and other nurses rushed Martha to the surgical unit...

Martha opened her eyes. She saw a silhouette of a man with a white coat and a big smile on his face. He asked her, "How are you feeling?"

Martha nodded back to him with a smile and teardrops rolled through her cheeks, glistening like a shining beacon of life!

THE OLD MAN AND MANNEQUIN

Samuel Houston was twenty-one years old when he was drafted into the Army. He was not happy to join the Army, as he was planning to finish his bachelor's degree in biology and then apply for medical school. He had been preparing for his medical school entrance examination, but with no warning, the draft board sent him a letter saying he has been selected by the Selective Service Commission and must join the Army to protect the country from Communists threatening to engulf South Vietnam.

Sam signed up for the Army and joined the basic training at Fort Bragg, North Carolina. It was June 1971. After a short basic training in a military operation Sam was sent to Vietnam. They built the American base camp close to a village called Nha Trang. The villagers welcomed the Americans and many volunteered to help the GIs clean their clothes and cook food. The Vietnamese developed a very cordial relationship with the young American GIs and provided a sense of family environment so they could overcome anxiety and stress in a war-torn country. The Americans hired many Vietnamese for building barracks and other construction projects. A few Vietnamese ladies worked in the camp doing various manual work. A Vietnamese girl named Thao worked in the barracks as a cook where Samuel Houston was posted. He liked the girl and fell in love with her. The girl also fell in love with Sam.

She was eighteen years old, light-skinned with brown eyes and dark black hair. She was a smart girl and learned to speak broken English with a deep Vietnamese accent. Sam taught her many common phrases and Americans slang. The girl taught Sam some important Vietnamese phrases which helped him to communicate with other villagers.

A villager noticed some strangers, probably members of Vietcong or sympathizers snooping around their village who might attempt to ambush the Americans. Thao heard about this information from the villager and mentioned to Sam. Sam notified the camp commander Major Tom Pitcher this information. Major Pitcher relayed this message to the headquarters and requested some additional tactical support for the camp.

It was a dark night, no moon in the sky as a cloud covered the new moon. Around 10 o'clock in the night a group of about five Vietcong members attacked the village with machine guns and grenades. They did not target the American camp, only the village because they felt it would be easy to neutralize a village supporting the American imperialist. Their attack on the village also would give warnings to other villagers stay away from Americans and not support them.

The villagers were in deep sleep. Only stray dogs barked seeing strangers around the village. The sound of machine-guns and exploding grenades woke villagers and everybody tried to lie down on the ground to take cover from the incoming bullets and grenades. American soldiers started firing their machine-guns to neutralize the attacking Vietcong. The whole village became an inferno as thatched houses burned. The fire shot up ten to fifteen feet high. An intense battle between American soldiers and Vietcong lasted about fifteen minutes;

the sounds of gunfire stopped and only the screams of humans could be heard across the village and the camp. The camp lit up like daylight as floodlights turned on. The medics split up into two groups. One group attended to the American soldiers who might have been shot, and the other group went to the village to attend to the wounded. Many villagers died; body parts and blood were scattered all over the village. Sam went to the house where the girl lived with her parents. He found the girls' parents had died, only she was alive with a gunshot wound to her left leg. Sam lifted her and ran to the medic to patch her up so she could be dispatched to the field hospital nearby. Sam prayed for the first time in his life and asked the Almighty to save her life.

The medic found a bullet pierced through her left thigh damaging no artery or bone structure. However, she lost more blood and went through a shock which left her unconscious. The medic stitched her and gave a shot to reduce pain and a heavy dose of antibiotics. Then they loaded her in the ambulance and took her to the field hospital. Major Pitcher ordered a band of GIs to search to see if any other Vietcong members were present in the vicinity.

The dawn arrived, and the sun spread its rays in a magnificent display of colors. The fire completely gutted the village. Thirty residents of the village died including adults and children. The smell of death along with bullet-ridden and charred bodies scattered all over the village. A band of vultures encircled the village.

Sam convinced the captain of his unit to let him go to the field hospital and see how the girl was doing. The captain gave him a pass to visit the hospital. He collected some wildflowers from the field and headed to the field hospital. The hospital comprised many tents. One set of tents was the female ward and the other set was the male ward. A nurse named Madeline escorted Sam to a tent where Thao lay on the bed. She was half asleep. Sam looked at her sublime face. Her lips were dry and pale because of blood loss and fear. The nurse tapped her shoulder; she opened her eyes and found Sam standing next to her bed. She burst into a smile and raised her arms to embrace Sam. He embraced her and kissed her temple with happiness. The girl in broken English said, "Sam I love you."

They released Thao from the field hospital and she went back to her burned village. The surviving village residents rebuilt their huts with help from the Americans. One of her surviving uncles took her into his home and family.

Sam's unit was transferred from Nha Trang to Pleiku, where Vietcong activity was intense. Sam could not tell the girl goodbye. It was a heartbreaking experience for Sam, but he knew that in a war life cannot dictate anything, only a ray of hope can keep you alive, as long as you could escape death which was lurking all around you. The intense desire to live can deny death as long as you anticipate the incoming grenade or flying bullets and duck a few milliseconds ahead of its targeted pathway.

Every passing day Sam felt he survived for another day. What would come next day was unknown, unpredictable, and uncertain. Every other night Sam and his squad mates went out on a search and destroy mission to kill Vietcong. There was a strict order from the Army that they would take no enemy VCs or NVAs as prisoners! The advance infantry training camp programed the recruits' mind to kill the enemy. If you did not kill your enemy, then the enemy would kill you. It was a choice you must carry with you in a war. It was always either you died or lived depending upon your decision. This brainwashing technique created fear that dictated survival and animalistic attitudes. During a night patrol Sam and his squad waited to ambush some enemy and kill them, so they could live for another day.

It was September 1972, and the war was winding down. The Americans at home protested against the war and were sick of wasting billions of dollars and hearing daily reports of death of over 50,000 young Americans. They convinced President Nixon that war with the North Vietnamese and Vietcong would not be won, and he needed to stop this carnage of American youth for nothing. So, on 27 January, 1973 President Nixon signed the Paris Peace Accord and started to withdraw American troops.

Sam received his release paper within thirty days after President Nixon signed the Paris Peace Accord. He along with his friend Jack Austin picked up a motorbike and headed to Nha Trang from Pleiku to search for the girl who he fell in love with during his stay in the campsite of Nha Trang. The dense jungle around Nha Trang campsite was almost bare because of Agent Orange. The village Xuong Huan was close to the Nha Trang campsite where Thao lived with her uncle's family. Sam and Jack entered the center of the village and looked for the thatched house where the girl lived. They found the house dilapidated and abandoned. Two years had passed by since Sam had been forced to move to Pleiku. Things had changed a lot. Sam was very depressed because he could not find the girl. They came across an old man who lived next to the girl's house and he told Sam Thao moved to the next village Van Thanh. Sam thanked the old man and gave him a pack of Camel cigarettes. The old man said, "Thank you and good luck."

Sam and Jack jumped on their motorbike and headed north to go to Van Thanh. The villagers were not happy to see two American men enter their village, but they knew Americans were leaving South Vietnam within few days. Two young men came close to them and Jack who knew Vietnamese, asked them if they could help them find where Thao was living. They knew Thao's family and gave them directions. Jack thanked them and gave them a pack of Camel cigarettes.

Sam parked the bike next to the house, then knocked on the wooden door. After a few minutes a young boy came to the door and opened it to see who was there. Jack asked the boy in Vietnamese, "Is Thao at home?"

The boy asked Jack. "What is your name?"

Jack looked at Sam then said, "Sam."

The boy moved from the door and went inside the house.

A few minutes later Thao came out and saw Sam standing in front of the door. Thao ran towards Sam and hugged him. Only tears merged to celebrate the union between two lovers after a long, torturous separation.

Thao asked Sam and Jack to come in. She introduced them to her uncle Linh and his wife Hong. Thao's aunty brought some food and drink. Uncle Linh asked Sam to bring the motorbike inside the house so that no one would steal the bike. It was a hot and humid day. Sam asked Thao to pack up some clothes and necessary articles in a bag so she could accompany him to Plieku, then catch a transporter plane to Bangkok, Thailand and get out of Vietnam. Thao asked her uncle Linh if she could join Sam and live with him. Uncle agreed to Thao's request because he knew Thao loved Sam. Also, it would be better for Thao to leave this village and go away with the Americans. Uncle Linh came close to Sam and held his hand and embraced him. He just said, "Take care of Thao, as she lost her parents on that dreaded night when five Vietcong guerrillas attacked the village. Thao was shot, and you helped her to go to the hospital and saved her life. I am very pleased to give her to your hand and heart, so you can protect and love her as long as you live."

Jack told Sam to take the motorbike and go as fast as possible to Pleiku. He would get a ride from another American soldier from Nha Trang camp. Both friends hugged each other. Jack said, "Take care and see you both in Los Angeles soon."

The war between Vietnam and Americans had ended but war between South Vietnam and North Vietnam was yet to be settled.

Sam picked up Thao and sat her on the backseat of the motorbike and sped away over an unpaved road as fast he could. Thao wrapped her hands around Sam's back so she could maintain balance without falling from the motorbike. Sam and Thao arrived at Pleiku late afternoon with no incident. The camp processed hundreds of American soldiers and their Vietnamese friends through military security office so they could catch military transport planes and be transferred to Bangkok, Thailand, where a massive camp would house American soldiers and Vietnamese refugees. The American government knew that those who supported an American army in the war would be prosecuted by the North Vietnamese and many would be tortured and jailed for life. The Pentagon created a Bureau of Immigration for American sympathizers who would receive special residency status in America. Any of these refugees would receive permanent residency in

America if an American citizen sponsored them. This way, America would pay back these people for their help and loyalty in this war.

Sam worked hard to convince the military immigration authority how Thao helped GIs by cooking and cleaning in the Nha Trang campsite. Vietcong guerrillas shot her for her loyalty to Americans. She played a crucial role in extracting important military intelligence from nearby villagers and passing it on to the Americans that some elements of Vietcong were around the Nha Trang campsite and might attempt to attack the garrison. They gave this information to Major Pitcher. This intelligence report prevented a direct attack by Vietcong on the camp. Sam's eloquent leadership and impeccable service in the infantry division impressed the immigration officer, and he granted a temporary permit for Thao to leave for America.

On February 20, 1973 Sam flew to Bangkok along with Thao, leaving Vietnam for good. They received temporary housing in the camp for soldiers and their Vietnamese friends in Prachinburi, a few miles away from Bangkok. In Prachinburi, the US built a massive camp for soldiers and refugees. Vietnamese refugees were vetted and interviewed to make sure they were not members/supporters of the Communist Party. Once political interviews were completed and refugees passed the thorough evaluation, then they had to go through batteries of medical tests such as tuberculin skin test, a blood test for sexually transmitted diseases to rule out syphilis, gonorrhea and other STDs. If all these tests were negative, then they were granted a temporary certificate of residency in the US for six months.

Three weeks after their arrival in Prachinburi camp, Sam

and Thao boarded a flight from Bangkok to Los Angeles, California. Thao had never seen a plane that huge in her life. It was a Boeing 707. She was at first scared to fly, but once the plane took off, she felt that she was a giant bird flying in the sky with absolute freedom. These feelings of free-spirited freedom she never knew existed. Never in life had she dreamed that she would leave her country and be with a man from America.

After almost twenty-four hours of flight they arrived in Los Angeles. Before arriving at Los Angeles their plane stopped in Paris, France for a layover of five hours. Then they boarded a separate plane from Paris to Los Angeles. Thao and Sam passed through the immigration with no problem, then picked up their belongings from the luggage track and headed to a motel close to the airport. Sam stayed three nights in Los Angeles for sightseeing and to shake off jet lag. For Thao airport highways, speeding cars and trucks looked so neat and clean, shining like a mirror — a Wonderland! She pinched her thigh to see if it was real or a dream filled with a fantasy that does not exist. During the long flight Sam asked if she would marry him. Thao said, "Yes, Sam, Yes." Then she held Sam in a tight embrace and cried.

A taxi-cab took Sam and Thao to a cheap hotel named "Paradise" a few miles from the airport. In the hotel registration book Sam wrote Samuel Houston (fiancé) and Thao Le (fiancée). The hotel front desk Clark looked at the register and smiled at both of them then winked at Sam. Sam opened the hotel room 207 with the key, then lifted Thao and carried her to the bed. He kissed her passionately, and she submitted to him with a loving smile.

The next morning Sam took Thao on a city tour and in the

evening, they walked holding hands on Hollywood Boulevard. After spending three nights in Los Angeles, Sam and Thao headed home to Atlanta, Georgia. They took a Greyhound bus to Atlanta; it took two days to reach Atlanta, but they enjoyed the long bus trip. They passed through mountains, valleys, riverbanks, and agricultural land that produced bountiful wheat, rice, fruits, and vegetables for everybody in America and the world.

Sam and Thao were married in a Presbyterian Church in Decatur, Atlanta. His family welcomed Thao into their family home in Decatur. He talked with the high school principal to see if Thao could enroll in the school so she could become proficient in the spoken and written English language. The principal of the school allowed Thao to attend school, and she started her class with eighth grade students. She was a smart girl, and she picked up the English language quickly. Then she wanted to finish high school, but the principal of the school told Sam that it would be better if Thao could study at home and prepare for the GED examination. The school board informed the principal of the school that an older student could not mix with younger students because of school board policy as set by the State of Georgia Education Department. Thao studied at home diligently and prepared to take the GED examination. After a year of hard work, Thao passed the GED examination and received a diploma showing completion of a high school equivalency. Then she enrolled in a community college to be a nurse. Sam also went back to the university to finish his bachelor's degree in biological sciences and studied for the Medical College Entrance Examination.

In May 1975 Thao gave birth to a baby boy. Sam named him John Houston. Their small family struggled financially, but they were very happy. In the summer of 1975, Sam received his bachelor's degree in biology. He got a job in a research laboratory as a technician helping his professor in a tissue culture laboratory. While he was working in the lab, he spent a lot of time studying for the medical school entrance examination so he could score high enough to be admitted into medical school. In May 1976 he received the notification from the Dean of Emory University Medical College that they had selected him to study medicine in the fall of 1976. They surprised Sam and he decided to attend Emory University.

Thao took over all the family responsibilities as Sam immersed himself in his studies and hospital rounds every day. Sam often told Thao that he could not fulfill his duties as a husband, father and a man of the house, but Thao always told him not to worry about these trivial things, just focus on his studies.

John turned five years old when Sam graduated from the medical school. After receiving his M.D. degree from the university, Sam joined a residency program in neurology, which was a four-year program. The stress and intensity of the program created a distance between Thao and Sam. But Thao held the ship together and raised John almost single handedly.

When John reached six years of age Thao enrolled him in elementary school. Every morning she took him to school by 7:30 am. Then at 3:15 pm she picked him up from the school. After school Thao sat with John to help him in his schoolwork. At bedtime she read some bedtime story so he could fall asleep. Sam came home late at night after finishing his rounds in the hospital. Often he did not come home at all, because of seventy-two-hour shift duty all medical residents had to go through. Thao felt she was missing closeness with Sam, but she sacrificed her pleasure to keep this marriage intact and struggled to overcome depression and loneliness. John also missed his father's absence, but Thao filled up the void through affection and tenderness.

Time passed by. Sam finished his residency program and took a job in Florida. The family moved to Orlando. Sam realized the time had come to pay attention to family welfare. He arranged a trip to Switzerland for one month. Sam booked flights on Delta from Atlanta to Zürich. They boarded the plane in Atlanta in the evening and arrived in Zürich in the morning where they went to the hotel near the railway station. They rested for a few hours. They strolled through the old town, stopped in Lindenhof Square to admire the architectural beauty of St. Peter's and Fraumunster churches, then walked along the shoulders of Lake Zurich.

Sam was holding Thao's hand and John was excitedly asking questions about some roads in the old town and why they were not smooth like roads in America. Sam had to explain that some of these cobblestone roads were built in medieval times and asphalt was not discovered yet.

All three started a new life by bonding together more since they had missed the last seven years. The beautiful scenery, mountains, lakes, and Swiss culinary delights filled with chocolates and fondue revived the sweetness of affection and tender love. It strengthened Sam and Thao's married life. The presence of their beloved son John also played an important role in removing gaps between his parents.

The next day they took the train to Lucerne. They stayed at Lucerne for three days. The first day they visited Chapel Bridge and the Lion Monument. The next day they hopped on a train from Lucerne to Alpnachstad, then they boarded the steepest cogwheel train in the world to the summit of the Mt. Pilatus. Driving up the mountain, the Alpine scenery was unforgettable. The summit was almost 7,000 feet above the sea level. Wildflowers were scattered around the valley. When the cogwheel train reached the summit, they got off the train and found themselves surrounded by the snowcapped peaks of Mt. Pilatus. The summit area was plastered with white wet snow. John scooped some snow, made a ball and threw it at his mother but it missed the target. Sam looked up, scooped some snow from the snow-covered embankment and rushed to Thao, grabbed her hand and smeared wet snow on Thao's face and embraced her. Thao giggled like a little girl to see her husband acting like a little child. John came close to his parents and hugged them with delight. It was a wonderful sight, a real reunion between Sam, Thao and John that was missing for a long time because of the demands of the stressful hospital work environment.

Coming back from the top of the mountain they took a cable ride on a gondola to reach Fragmuntegg then Kriens. All got off at Kriens cable car station, walked through the little town and then boarded a postal bus to go to the Kriens railway station. From there they boarded a train going to Lucerne. The trip was fabulous and the Alpine fresh air invigorated everyone. John could hardly wait to go to Mount Titlis the next day.

John woke up when it was still dark. He was excited to see Mt Titlis because Sam told him it was better than Mt. Pilatus. All headed to the railway station then boarded on a train heading to Engelberg, which was less than one hour from Lucerne. From Engelberg they boarded the "Titlis XPress" gondola. When they reached the summit, they found they were surrounded by snowcapped mountain peaks on all sides. The panoramic view was astonishingly pretty and difficult to describe. They were on the top of the clouds as if they were floating on them. Then they walked into the Glacier Cave, a tunnel in the ice of glacier. The altitude of Mt. Titlis was 10,623 feet.

The next day they started their journey to Bern, the capital of Switzerland, in the afternoon the train took them from Lucerne to Bern within an hour and a half. They strolled around the old town filled with fountains and statues depicting stories of Bible and important people during biblical times. They visited the Rose Garden, Berner Munster (Bern Cathedral) and the famous eight-hundred-year-old clock tower. It fascinated both John and Thao to see the appearance of the jumping figurines just four minutes before the hour strikes the bell. John asked his father if he could get an electric train set for his birthday next year. Sam said, "I will buy you a toy train for your birthday if you study hard."

Visiting the mighty Matterhorn was the next item on the itinerary. They took a train from Bern to go to Zarmatt which lay at the foot of the mighty Matterhorn — one of the highest mountain peaks in Europe. They boarded a train from Bern to Visp railway station, then got off at Visp and boarded another train from Visp to Zarmatt. Zarmatt was a small village where no automobiles were allowed. Instead people got around by horse drawn carriages. The scenery and beauty of the little town, its roads, and people moving around looked like a magic kingdom. The air was crisp and invigorating. They stayed two nights there.

The next stop was St. Moritz, the playground of rich and

famous people. They reserved seats for the famous Glacier Express which took a long seven and half hours to reach the final destination. The train moved slowly but as steadily as a magical serpent opening the window of panoramic views of magnificent Alpine passes, cliffs, winding viaducts, tunnels, deep gorges, ravines and bridges. The amazing, incredible sights and sounds would be etched in the mind's eye forever.

The family spent two nights at St. Moritz, enjoyed the opulence and extravagant living for a few days as an outsider, trying to take a peek at the lifestyle of the rich and famous people of the world. The next stage of their travel plan included Lausanne, Château de Chillon and Geneva. In the early morning they boarded a train from St. Moritz to Chur, then got off at Chur, and boarded a train headed to Zurich. They stayed at Zurich for the night.

This hopping around from one train to the next was an exciting experience for John. He loved every moment of this wonderful rail journey and said, "I will cherish this experience all my life." The next day they took the train to Lausanne. The family stayed three nights at Lausanne because they were a little tired of extensive travel and did nothing but walk in the park close to Lake Geneva.

A local train from Lausanne took them to Veytaux-Chillon railway station. After getting off from the train they walked a short distance to reach the Chateau de Chillon castle on the shore of Lake Geneva. It was a beautiful castle, spacious with great halls, a chapel filled with beautiful paintings and murals. Beside all these beautiful paintings and glittering dining halls to feed and entertain Royals and Dukes, it had a cavernous dungeon to torture and kill people who were against the Christian church. Many women who did not agree with the church's dictums were branded as witches and burned alive in the dungeon. Human bones were scattered around the dungeon chambers. These bones could not speak but carried vicious and torturous secrets for future inhabitants of this castle. Seeing the scattered bones deep inside the semi dark chambers, John screamed in fear and hid his face in his mother's bosom. Thao gripped her son and consoled him not to be afraid then she said, "Let us move to the upper chambers of the Castle. These chambers are musty and damp."

The next day they arrived at Geneva from Lausanne, which was only less than an hour's drive. In Geneva they visited the famous fountain, the European headquarters of the United Nations and Red Cross. They strolled around the park on the shores of Lake Geneva and came across many beautiful sculptures. They went back to their hotel. Thao thanked Sam for this wonderful time spent together in Switzerland filled with natural wonders and scenic beauty unparalleled in this planet. She would cherish this experience as long as she lived. Sam responded, "Because your presence and beauty made these experiences more alluring and memorable to me." They kissed each other then all three held their hands forming a circle and danced in the room. This dancing circle represented the eternity!

In April 1985, nine years since the birth of John Thao became pregnant again. Both husband and wife became happy after this long wait to have another child. John learned that he would soon have a brother or sister to play with. He was happy he wrote in his journal. "I will have a sister soon. I can hardly wait to welcome her into our home." He wanted a sister only, no brother. In January 1986 Thao gave birth to a baby girl. She asked John what name he would like to give her. John replied, "Lisa." Sam and Thao liked the name, so Lisa Houston became a new member of the Houston family.

Twenty-five years had passed by. Sam became a well-respected, successful neurologist. Thao went back to school, received her bachelor's degree in nursing, and then became an administrator at a hospital. John finished his law degree and became a partner in a well-known law farm in Tampa, Florida. Lisa finished her Master's degree in science education and became a teacher in a high school in Orlando. The whole family became a loving, caring model family for other families to emulate.

It was Christmas season. Thao and Sam went to pick up the Christmas tree from a nearby plant dealer. They selected a beautiful pine tree about six feet tall and placed it in the middle of the spacious living room. Thao, Sam, John, and Lisa placed various ornaments and tinsel on the tree. John placed tiny light bulbs around the tree and an Angel on the top of the tree. When the tree was completely dressed up, John turned on the switch. The whole living room became a bright, shining place filled with joy and happiness.

On Christmas Day Sam invited some friends for a dinner party. The house was full of people; everybody enjoyed the hospitality of the Houston family. When all the guests left Sam and Thao retired to their bedroom. Thao, holding Sam's hand said, "Sam I have noticed a lump on my left breast. It is tender and very sensitive." Sam loosened her silk kimono and touched her breast to feel the lump. He also noticed the lump. The nipple showed some discoloration and a slight secretion oozed out from it. Both knew that some bad things were coming their way. Sam kissed his wife and said, "Don't worry;

everything will be all right." Thao did not say a word, only her eyes welled up and tears flooded Sam's face.

The next morning Sam took Thao to his friend Dr. Smith who was the chief oncologist in the department of Oncology in the hospital. He asked Sam to have a diagnostic mammogram and some blood tests done on Thao in the imaging center. The following day the result of the mammogram came. Dr. Smith look at the mammogram and read the results from the laboratory report then said, "Thao has two small tumors in the breast tissue each about 1 cm wide. We need a biopsy of the tumor tissue to know if the tissue is cancerous." Dr. Smith continued, "Take Thao to the hospital and admit her as an outpatient so that the surgeon could do a needle biopsy on her breast and armpit lymph nodes. Chemical, immunologic and anatomical tests should be done so we can know for sure if the tumors are cancerous."

Sam and Thao both were very familiar with cancer, but the impact of the disease was less on you until it affected your own family or self. The fear of death dominated the mind, body and the whole existence. It created an environment of doom and hopelessness, which took away human happiness and contentment, and left behind a sense of despair and uncertainty which consumed you and your existence.

Next day Dr. Keating, a general surgeon conducted biopsy of the tumors and lymph nodes and sent the tissue for chemical, immunologic and anatomical tests to various clinical laboratories. Three days later Dr. Smith called Sam to come with Thao to the hospital to get results of the biopsy and immunologic analysis. Sam was very nervous and felt that his entire world of happiness was about to crash. The nurse called both to follow her in the room and wait for Dr. Smith to come.

After twenty minutes of anxiously waiting for Dr. Smith to come in, the door opened and Dr. Smith entered the room. He shook Thao's and Sam's hands then said, "I am sorry to inform you that Mrs. Houston has an aggressive form of estrogen positive cancer, which has metastasized in her body. The lymph nodes are all affected and cancer cells have infiltrated in various organs. The team of oncologists reviewed Mrs. Houston's case and recommended that the left breast must be completely removed and chemo and radiation therapies must be simultaneously administered immediately."

Sam sat there silently for a few seconds then said, "Dr. Smith, is this treatment protocol best for Thao to follow?" Dr. Smith replied, "It is the only treatment available for Mrs. Houston." Thao sat there without a word, only holding Sam's hand tightly. Tears rolled down Sam's eyes. Thao wiped Sam's tears and said, "Sam have faith in science." Dr. Smith got up and held Thao's hand and said, "Mrs. Houston I am very sorry to tell you this bleak, and shocking prognosis, but I have absolute confidence in you and that you are capable of beating this disease."

Thao looked straight at Dr. Smith and said, "Yes, we will beat this disease. I thank you for your help."

Thao was driving the car; she didn't show any emotion. It devastated Sam to hear Dr. Smith's prognosis. He cried like a child who had just lost his precious toy. After arriving home Thao told her husband, "Don't worry. We have come across death and other insurmountable challenges before and together we have overcome all these obstacles. This time we will fight together against all odds and we will win this battle."

Sam kissed his wife and with a melancholic voice said, "Thao, I cannot live without you because you are my strength and soulmate."

Thao whispered, "I feel the same way, Sam."

The following Monday Thao was admitted to the hospital for surgery. Sam sat in the waiting room during surgery and prayed to God to save Thao's life. The surgery lasted three hours when the effects of anesthesia wore off, and the nurse called Sam to follow her to the post-operative room. Thao was half asleep on the bed. Sam kissed her on the temple and she opened her eyes to see Sam standing next to her bed. She smiled at him. The operating surgeon came to Sam and said, "Everything went well; your wife is a brave girl." Sam thanked the surgeon.

The surgeon placed a tube on the chest wall to drain the fluid out. After three day's stay in the hospital Dr. Smith discharged Thao from the hospital. Sam brought her home. He hired a lady nurse to come home twice a day to take care of Thao.

Sam resumed his practice only three days in a week, so he could devote more time to Thao. Radiation and chemotherapy lasted for one month, but doctors found no improvement in her condition. A diagnostic MRI revealed multiple spots that were not present before showing the cancerous tissue spreading rapidly in her body. Sam would sit with her for hours and feed her during the day and at nighttime. Thao lost over thirty pounds within two months and she developed chronic diarrhea. Sam realized Thao had little time to live. Every day she looked thinner than the previous day. Sam and the children sat around Thao's bed and talked with her whenever she wanted. Often Thao asked John and Lisa to look after their dad, as she prepared for her departure from this earth to an unknown space.

Thao always smiled when she talked with her children, but nowadays that beautiful smile had disappeared from her dry lips, as if some unknown force stole that unique characteristics from her. Sam also forgot how to smile. Gloom and melancholy covered the room as if death was waiting for her outside.

Thao developed a bout of hiccups in the evening. Sam called a doctor for a house visit. The doctor gave some shots to control this spasmodic breathing condition. The treatment intermittently stopped the hiccups but early in the morning hiccups returned with a vengeance. Sam knew the time has come Thao would leave him forever. After an hour the hiccups stopped, but the lungs could not withstand this trauma anymore. She passed away.

Sam went back to his neurology practice, but he felt that he lacked the energy and mental strength to continue this profession. His colleagues noticed Sam was depressed, often forgetting words and having a little trouble thinking of the right words, showing some memory loss.

One of his neurologist friends Dr. Sinha suggested a neurological evaluation because he knew Sam had extensive exposure to Agent Orange defoliants in Vietnam. Dr. Sinha suspected Sam's condition had a direct link to the effects of Agent Orange. Sam went to a neurologist Dr. Rice for a checkup. She conducted various neurological tests including laboratory blood work. The result showed Sam had developed slight dementia.

Sam quit his practice. His health became an issue with him. He developed muscle weakness, often forgetting the names of places and objects he was familiar with, and mood changes. John was very worried seeing his dad's downward physical and mental conditions. He called Dr. Sinha and explained to him his father's conditions. Dr. Sinha knew John very well as he often visited their home. After hearing John's description of his father's condition, he asked John if he could arrange a trip to Switzerland where the whole family stayed together and bonded. Then Dr. Sinha asked John to report to him whether Sam could remember the good times they had in Zürich and Mt. Pilatus. He also asked John not to tell anything to his father about this discussion regarding this experiment.

John and Lisa planned a trip to Switzerland in June. Both thought it will be good for their dad. Sam always talked about their vacation in various places in Europe and South America, particularly the time they spent in Switzerland. John and Lisa told Sam their plan to visit Switzerland in June and he agreed, then said, "It will be good to have a change in life."

They boarded a plane from Atlanta to Zürich, Switzerland. As planned, they went from Zürich to Mt. Pilatus via cable car. The scenery was beautiful. On the top of the mountain there was a café where they drank coffee and ate some snacks. Outside the café snow was everywhere. John scooped up some snow, made a ball with snow and threw at Lisa. Lisa scooped up some snow and threw it at her dad. Sam smiled at Lisa and scooped up some wet snow and smeared it on Lisa's face and uttered, "Thao!"

Lisa realized her dad was thinking of her mother and transposing Lisa as Thao. John was waiting for this moment because this memory was vivid in his dad's mind. John remembered his dad scooped wet snow and smeared on his mother's face in the same spot on top of Mount Pilatus, thirty-five years ago. Only difference was his mother Thao was absent here. But his father was hallucinating his wife's presence through the images of Lisa!

Lisa asked her dad, "How did you like the trip?" Sam replied, "I enjoyed the trip but some cities I have seen for the first time." This answer showed to John that his father had lost some memory. John contacted Dr. Sinha and gave a detailed description of the trip with a special emphasis on the Mount Pilatus events. After hearing John's detailed report Dr. Sinha told him his father was suffering from mixed dementia. Then he said, "I will contact Dr. Rice so she can develop a treatment plan for your dad."

A week after their trip to Switzerland Dr. Rice called Sam to have a brain scan so they could pinpoint what was causing the dementia and selective memory loss. Sam was not happy to hear that he needed to have a brain scan done. John convinced his dad to go through this test and Sam reluctantly agreed to his son's request.

Dr. Rice requested an 18F- FDG positron emission tomography scan to see if there was an impairment of metabolic activity in the parietal lobe of the brain. The result of the scan showed a distinct impairment of metabolic activities so Sam was suffering from Alzheimer's disease and/or Lewy Body Dementia. There was no medicine available to reverse this aggressive dementia.

Sam's condition worsened as days passed by. He experienced memory loss, muscle weakness, started forgetting names, showing impulsive behavior and searching everywhere for Thao. Dr. Sinha suggested to John that a mannequin might help Sam calm down and reduce his impulsive behavior and help to improve his long-term memory. It upset John to hear Dr. Sinha's suggestion, but he realized it might be the only treatment that could help his father. Dr. Sinha wrote a prescription for this experiment and John ordered a female mannequin for his father. Dr. Sinha reminded John of the incident at Mount Pilatus when they were traveling in Switzerland few years back.

Lisa moved to the parents' home and hired a certified patient caretaker to look after her dad when she went to her school teaching job. The young caretaker Pam came home in the morning and left late afternoon five days a week. Pam cooked for the family and helped Sam with whatever he needed. During weekends John came home from Tampa and looked after his father.

A female mannequin arrived at Sam's house. Lisa pulled out a blue silk kimono her mother loved to wear from the dresser and put that on the mannequin. Then she placed the mannequin on her parents' bed and covered it under a thin blanket.

In the night Sam entered his room and lifted the bed cover to lie down. He noticed Thao was sleeping next to his bed. Sam kissed and embraced her. Lisa watched her dad's reaction through the security camera. After a few minutes Sam fell asleep.

The next morning Lisa greeted her father. Sam smiled at her and said, "I found Thao hiding in my bed." Lisa was happy to see her father in a good mood. Pam was making some pancakes and omelets for breakfast. Sam placed a pancake on the plate and moved to his bedroom. Lisa saw her father was trying to feed the mannequin by opening its mouth. A few minutes later Sam came out of his bedroom and said, "Thao is not eating food. She is not hungry." Then he left the dining table and started to talk to himself meaning less rubbish. Pam came close to him and said, "Food is served, so please eat your food." Then she held his hand and sat him on his chair in the dining table. Sam ate some pieces of pancake, but kept on repeating, "Thao is not eating."

Sam's physical/mental condition deteriorated rapidly. He talked a lot, walked around the house and a backyard with a gait and repeated, "I have to be home to see Thao." Doctors gave some medicine to control the progression of dementia but Alzheimer's vicious tentacles sucked out the cognitive domain of Sam's brain.

It was Sunday morning when John went to his dad's bedroom to see how he was doing. He found his dad was holding the mannequin and he was in a deep sleep. He did not wake up his dad and left the room. It was around 10 o'clock and Sam did not wake up. Lisa went in the room and found her dad holding the mannequin and asleep. She tried to wake him but Sam did not respond—the body was cold. Lisa screamed frantically and called John to come to their dad's room. John came running, touched Sam's body, and he realized that his father was dead. He called 911. The ambulance came and medical technicians gave CPR but there was no response, then the ambulance rushed to the hospital emergency room. The attending physician checked the patient and pronounced the patient dead!

CAMP DACHAU

A well-respected electrician named Klaus Heinrich lived in a small township in the Munich area with his wife Edith, who was an elementary school teacher in Munich. They had two children Josef and Angelika. Josef was a sixteen-year-old, handsome, strong young man who loved to play soccer. He was also a God-fearing German protestant. His sister Angelika was eight years old, had blue eyes, and a sharp nose with freckles all over her pretty face. She loved to draw pictures.

In 1939 Hitler with his Nazi party, supported by thousands of young fanatics, snatched central power in Germany and declared himself as the Chancellor of Germany. All young German lads aged fourteen to eighteen were fascinated by the outcry of German nationalism and the appearance of the Third Reich that would soon avenge the humiliating defeat of Germany during the World War I. All young boys must join and become members of the Nazi party and be known as Hitler Jugend (HJ).

The electrician's family never cared about the national politics; they were interested only in their own work and having a healthy and prosperous family life. Josef dreamed of being a medical doctor when he grew up. The political reality brought a turmoil in all of Germany, and it shook every family. Almost all the young neighbors of Josef became members of the Nazi party. His friends wanted him to join the party but

Josef never felt the urge to join with these young fanatic groups. His friends abandoned him and called names, taunting him as a coward and anti-social. Josef was sad to see that his close friends rejected him. He became a loner and isolated himself from everybody.

One day Klaus was drinking beer with some fellow villagers in a beer hall. He drank a lot of beer and got drunk. When he was drunk, he said to his fellow neighbors that the Nazi party would ruin Germany and the country would pay for this madness. All of his friends tried to keep Klaus's mouth shut, but he kept on blabbering. Everybody became alarmed, and one villager punched Klaus in his face so he would stop talking. Blood came gushing from Klaus's mouth and he fell on the ground and passed out. His friends carried him home.

Gunter Ritter punched Klaus because he realized Klaus was endangering his own life and perhaps, all the people close to him. There were rumors everywhere that Nazi party loyalists were looking for people who were against the party and hunting them down so that the party supremacy would be absolute. Anybody disobeying or questioning the party's authority would receive hard labor and other sorts of punishment.

A few days went by since the incident in the beer hall and Klaus was afraid that somebody might notify the Nazi party and it might bring a lot of trouble for his whole family. But nothing happened for over a week, so Klaus felt a little better and relieved that trouble might be over. A month later in the middle of the night somebody knocked on Klaus's front door. He was asleep, and he took some time to open the door. It shocked him to see a Gestapo man accompanied by a villager. The Gestapo officer asked, "Are you Klaus Heinrich?"

Klaus felt a sharp chill ran through his spine, and with a mumble he said, "I am Klaus Heinrich."

The Gestapo stretched his club and rested it on Klaus's shoulder, then with a scream he said, "You scoundrel, get out of the house, pack your bag with your family and report to the railway center of the SS office of registration tomorrow morning at nine." Klaus was petrified but tried to talk with the Gestapo officer to find out why he had to report to the Office of Registration. The officer thought for a second then said, "You pig, just follow my orders."

The next day Klaus family went to the registration office in Munich, as the Gestapo officer ordered him to do. The commandant of the registration office asked Klaus his name, address, profession/skills he possessed. Klaus provided all this information to the commandant. At this point Josef interrupted his father and said to the commandant, "Please forgive my father. He made a big mistake of saying bad things against the Nazi party because he was drunk. I dislike my father because of his anti-Nazi sentiment. I am ready to join the Nazi party and happy to serve my fatherland."

The articulation of Josef impressed the commandant and he was lenient to Klaus and Edith for their crime against the state. He told Josef to see the commandant of the Nazi party next day. Klaus and Edith were given a stern warning and released. This repudiation from his son shocked Klaus and Edith and both of them felt humiliated and betrayed by their own flesh and blood. Klaus was speechless and Edith burst out sobbing. They could not understand why their beloved son Josef would say something so bad against their own family.

The close-knit Klaus family fell apart like shattered glass. Edith could not understand why Josef behaved like this. She had raised Josef and Angelika to be sweet and nice, well behaved and respectful to family and friends. She was petrified and clueless. Edith started to doubt herself and her ability to bring up her children. She wondered what the country was becoming. Klaus and Josef came back home but Josef did not say a word to his father and mother. Klaus and Edith did not feel to talk to Josef, for his behavior stunned and deeply hurt them.

The next morning Josef went to the Nazi party headquarters in Munich to meet the commandant of the youth corps, filled in details of family information, signed the membership form and took an oath of allegiance to the Nazi party. He became a member of Hitler Jugend. The following day they took him to the Grunewald Camp for basic training. After three months of basic training they selected him to join the physical fitness, operating rifles, and other special cadet programs for advanced military training corps where cadets learned how to use antitank weapons and tactical warfare. Every day they underwent routine marches with full combat gear. He learned the theory and practice of many weapons used in combat and became an expert sharpshooter. Because of his hard work ethics, intelligence and loyalty to his superiors, Josef became a favorite Hitler Jugend and was promoted to a leadership position in Hitler's youth corps.

Josef returned home after one year of training in the Hitler Jugend advanced camp. He was wearing his Hitler Jugend uniform and knocked on the door. Edith opened the door and found Josef standing with his uniform. She hugged him, and tears welled up her pretty face. Mother and son hold each other for some time then, Edith asked, "How have you been? "Josef said in a whisper, "I am doing well."

Edith said, "Change your clothes and come to the kitchen to eat some porridge and cheese," then she handed him some clothes. Joseph did not utter a word, only his tears flooded his cheek that expressed his year-long separation from his family and anguish that embedded in his heart, mind, and soul.

Josef took a shower and dressed in his own house clothes and sat at the kitchen table. Edith look at him in silence then said, "Why did you put your family down in front of the commandant in the registration center? How could you do that Josef? All our family values crashed in front of everybody?"

Josef raised his head, then said, "Mama I had to do that so that the commandant would leave my dad alone, and not send him in Dachau camp, where people have no place to go except to meet death!"

Edith looked at her son with tears in her eyes and said, "Now I know why you did that. It mortified me to hear your derogatory words against your father, and I could not believe that you could do that kind of thing."

Josef went to his mother and held her and said, "Mama I will never shame you and our family. I want you to believe in me. I promise you that justice will be done in due time."

In the evening the family gathered around Josef in the kitchen asking many questions about the life at the Hitler Jugend campsite. Josef gave a detailed routine of activities in the camp then he said, "Don't trust your neighbors. Whatever I have said here should not go outside our house. A new internal political police (Streifendienst) is everywhere. They're looking for people who are anti-Nazi party and/or critical about the philosophy of Nazism and Hitler's vision of a Third Reich. Once they identify them, they would be locked up and sent to the camps for protective custody and labeled — anti-nationalist Germans. So never talk with your neighbors, friends, and acquaintances about political conditions in Germany. You must hide your honest opinion; only speak of the great achievements of the Nazi party and Hitler's vision for Germany."

Before leaving home, Josef embraced his sister Angelika and said, "Be careful of the boys of Jungvolk. They are devils."

Angelika answered, "I will be careful."

Josef left home after a week and joined his HJ comrades. His face showed a different expression where sorrow and sadness mixed with a determination made a stoic appearance filled with great resolve.

Edith noticed Josef had changed a lot since he left home after the incident in the commandant's office a year ago. Klaus felt the same, but could not figure out what was happening to him. The HJ camp activities and Nazi party cadres had changed the outlook of life for him.

It was March 1938. Hitler annexed Austria and Sudetenland (western part of Czechoslovakia), and war drums were beating faster for the emergence of the Third Reich — the goal of the Nazi party in Germany. The members of Hitler Jugend prepared for the war machine that the Nazi party instituted in Germany. Josef realized his time was running out as an elite member of HJ and he must make his plan work before it engulfed him in the looming fire of war.

To celebrate the Fuhrer Hitler's birthday on April 20 in 1938 a huge gathering assembled in a football stadium in Munich. Many advanced tanks were there to show off the German military might, national pride and readiness to bring the former glory of Germanic people which was quashed in the First World War defeat in Versailles. Besides military parades and high-stepping goose march, one special event was arranged to show off the marksmanship of elite cadets of HJ members. The best marksman would receive a special medal from General Gottlob Berger, Commander of the SS-Hauptant. General Kurt Gruber, First Chairman of Hitler Jugend would also be present to cheer his young troops.

They selected the five best marksmen from the whole of Germany, and Josef was one of the best rifle marksmen in the country. He represented Munich district as the best all-rounder cadet among HJ members. The commander of his unit Major Erik Schmidt recommended Josef as the most promising leader in HJ Corps and predicted in due time he would become a full-fledged major in the army. Joseph had the ability to shoot any object with the rifle fifty meters away. He earned the best marksmanship award in all of Munich.

They thoroughly searched each HJ cadet selected for the marksmanship contest before lining them up in the shooting area. Each candidate received a magazine containing three bullets and could only fire three shots in the target board. The person who hit the center dot most often in the board and received the highest points would win the contest. The judges would decide who hit the target in the center most often and declare that person as the winner of the contest.

The first cadet, Ben, received the rifle from the judge and loaded his gun with a magazine containing three bullets. He fired a first shot which hit the target board in the third circle away from the center dot. The second shot was a little away from the center and third hit the center red dot. The target judge took the board away from the line and kept it for further evaluation and analysis. A group of three judges would test each target board and tabulate the scores. Cadet Jones was next. The target judge placed a new board and the firing judge asked cadet Jones to come to the firing line and start shooting. The first shot hit the center red dot, then he fired a second shot that also hit the center red dot. The third shot hit a far corner of the second circle of the target board. The target judge looked at the board and set it aside for evaluation. Cadet Finn was the third member on the list. He came forward to the firing line and aimed at the target, pulling the trigger. The bullet hit center circle a few centimeters away from the red dot. The next shot hit the center red dot. Everybody waited for the final shot. Finn pulled the trigger, and the bullet hit the center red dot. The crowd roared. He was confident that he would win the prize.

The fourth cadet Paul approached the firing line and pulled the trigger. The bullet hit the center of the red dot. The next shot hit the second circle of the board and the third shot also hit the outer most circle. He was very disappointed about his performance. He looked down and walked away from the firing line. The last candidate Josef came to the firing line. The line judge handed over the rifle to him. He checked the magazine, looked at the surroundings for a second then focused at the shooting target and fired his first shot. The bullet went straight at the center red dot and made a nice hole in the center. The crowd burst into applause. The field coordinator raised his flag and signaled the crowd to be silent. Josef, standing erect looked at the target board, then suddenly moved his aim to the front line of the dignitaries' row, and fired a shot straight at General Gottlob Berger's head, then fired the remaining bullet at the chest of General Kurt Gruber. Two shots hit the targets, and both generals fell to the floor. Blood splattered all over and made the ground red.

Three SS guards were standing close to the firing line. They ran towards Josef and fired at him. Josef fell on the ground. Blood gushed out from his head, chest, and shoulder as all three revolvers emptied their load on his body. Before his last breath Josef said with hatred, "Hitler ist ein Schwein."

There was pandemonium in the Stadium. The SS/SA security police covered the area where the two generals lay in the field bleeding profusely. A couple of doctors attending the generals trying to stop bleeding. The military ambulances came and rushed the generals to the hospital. Ambulances arrived at the hospital and took both generals to the surgical unit and tried to revive them but due to excessive blood loss both were pronounced dead within a few minutes after their arrival in the surgical unit.

SS men stopped each person in attendance in the stadium, searched them and recorded their name, address and other information before they allowed them to leave the stadium. It shocked everybody in the stadium to see how a single HJ cadet would disrupt the organized event like this. SS officers dragged Josef's bullet ridden dead body to a military truck and moved away to the nearby military barracks. The SS men muffled completely the news of assassination and they ordered a curfew to prevent similar armed activities by the anti-Nazi elements in Munich and whole country.

In the middle of the night a group of SS men with machine guns kicked the front door open at Klaus's home. They dragged Klaus and Edith from their bedroom and screamed at them, "You swine now you must die." Then shoved them into the military truck, loaded with other people. One SS officer pulled Angelika's hair and dragged her to the same truck. People in the truck were all shocked because intense fear of death mortified them and made them speechless and frozen. Angelika sobbed in her mother's embrace. No one knew why they had been tortured by their own countrymen with no cause or reason.

The military truck picked up a few more people from neighboring cities then proceeded in the northwest direction toward Dachau. The German government had built this camp Dachau for German citizens who opposed the Nazi rule. About an hour and a half hour later the truck arrived at Dachau. They dragged all the prisoners out from the truck and directed them to form lines. The camp filled with cries from children, clutching their mothers' bodies. Once the formation of the lines was complete, the officer approached the line and asked each person their name, address, and other details. An assistant of the officer then recorded the information in a book. Once all information was recoded, the officer moved to the next person. When the officer approached Klaus, he asked him, "What is your name and address?"

Klaus responded, "Klaus Heinrich. Frustenrieder Starabe 53, Munich." The officer pulled his pistol from the holster, looked at him with a menacing stare then asked, "Are you related to Josef Heinrich?"

Klaus replied, "He is my son."

"You bastard; I will shoot you right now." The sergeant following the captain came close to the officer and whispered that Major General Glucks wanted to talk to Klaus Heinrich. From a distance Edith saw the captain pointing the gun at Klaus. She closed Angelika's eyes and prayed, "God please save Klaus."

The captain moved his pistol from Klaus's face. Two SS guards came forward, grabbed Klaus's arms and dragged him to a truck and moved him to the other side of the camp.

The captain moved to the next person in the line and asked the same question about their name, address, and other information. Edith thanked God for saving Klaus from immediate death. She was wondering why the Gestapo was so mad about their family. What did Klaus do to them that brought so much hatred and anger? She could not figure it out. Only she realized that something would happen to her family that would destroy their life. She prayed to God to save her husband and daughter Angelika from these vicious killers. She was not afraid to die and would sacrifice her life if that would prevent these killers from harming her family.

They put handcuffs on Klaus and then they took him to the commandant's office for interrogation. Commandant Major General Glucks asked many questions about Josef, who were his friends and what he talked about when he was visiting home. What did he say about the Nazi party and the youth camp when he was posted there? Klaus said, "He discussed nothing in the house when he came back home for a brief visit, after almost one year of absence." A junior officer handed a dossier that contained information about Klaus and Josef to Commandant Glucks. He looked critically the file then asked, "Klaus why did you get involved in anti-Nazi propaganda in a beer hall next to St Jakob's-Platz?"

"I was drunk and complained against the party because the price of beer doubled. I am sorry and I beg the Commandant's forgiveness. It will never happen again," replied Klaus. Then the Major General asked Klaus, "What is your profession?"

Klaus replied, "I am a master electrician."

Commandant Glucks closed the file and ordered him to join the squad of electricians to assemble and set up electrical fence around the camp. They placed Edith and Angelika in the female housing sector.

They housed very few families with small children in the camp, if the husband and wife were important members in Social Democratic Party and, Communist Party. In this area the Communist Party organization was very strong and influential in Munich, and the Nazis hated the Communists because they challenged the Nazi party for controlling all of Germany. They allowed some families with children to work as maids or housekeepers in family houses in the city of Dachau. Edith was placed in a home as a tutor of two children, because Nazis valued the teachers. Angelika lived in the camp with Edith. Edith also worked at the camp's clothing shop where uniforms for the German army were made. There were four or five children aged five to ten years old in the camp. Angelika would play with them, read short stories, and often busily draw on a slate Edith received from the family for whom she tutored.

The camp needed electricians for developing extensive electrical wiring to all the newly built barracks, and other office buildings. Also, they had to develop a network of high-voltage electrical fences that would deter prisoners from escaping from the camp. Klaus was a master electrician, and he was responsible for setting up the electrical fencing system in Dachau camp. He hated his work but just to keep himself out of trouble, he just followed orders. Torture and humiliation stripped away human resistance that clouded their judgment regarding what was right and what was wrong. Klaus also joined hundreds of other prisoners who lost their ability to stand up against oppression; they just followed the masters and submitted to them as lifeless human existence.

Hitler's army invaded Poland in September 1939 and hundreds of Polish Communists and resistance fighters were arrested and shipped to Dachau concentration camp. The condition of the camp became worse because of the huge influx of people overwhelming the food supply system, overcrowding, and creating an unsanitary condition and food shortage that led to starvation. They forced prisoners to hard labor which led to many deaths because of lack of food, poor health, and sheer exhaustion. Many committed suicide, by jumping on the electrified barbed wire and many got shot while attempting to escape.

Klaus came across Sheeler, a neighbor, and a member of the Communist Party, who was hiding from Nazis in a village far from Dachau, but the Gestapo found out the village where he was hiding. They arrested him and sent him to Dachau to do hard labor for the country. Sheeler heard about the assassination of two generals by Josef Heinrich. He told Klaus his son Josef killed Generals Gottlob and Gruber during the best marksmanship competition. SS guards killed Josef during the shootout. It stunned Klaus to hear that Josef was dead. He could not cry because seeing death every day and living among death took away the basic emotion of humans to express the sadness, melancholy, and tears for the passing of a loved one. The teardrops dried out; only the sigh expressed its existence as breathing continued to hold on to its function.

Every morning by six o'clock all prisoners came out from the barracks and stood in line for roll call. After roll call they proceeded to the canteen for some bread, coffee and half a cup of potato soup. Then they marched out to the nearby factory to make cabinets, rifles, or caskets. Some prisoners were trucked away to the nearby mountain range to collect blasted boulders and crush them into small pieces of rocks and pebbles with a hammer. These pebbles made roads. They worked nonstop for twelve hours with no food or rest. Many succumbed to this hard labor and passed away. The dead bodies lay on the roadside as the fodder for wild animals and vultures to consume.

Hitler's war machine marched on like a thunder from Czechoslovakia, Poland, Denmark and Norway, it uprooted millions of people; thousands died at the front, and thousands more were loaded into trains of cattle boxcars like a herd of animals and sent to various concentration camps around Dachau. Many died in the cattle boxcars in transit. Life became a meaningless entity, death lurking around all corners of the camp like hyenas licking their bloodthirsty lips with ecstasy.

Klaus and Sheeler together planned to build a small radio from scraps so they could hear some news coming from partisan clandestine broadcasts. Sheeler bribed a Kapo named Christoph Kruger to get a radio for him from the town. Kapos were German criminals who assisted SS guards in the camp. Some of these criminals were vicious, and a sadistic group of deranged people who enjoyed torture and other physical abuses of the internees. Sheeler told Christoph if he could get some parts for a radio then he would give him money so he could enjoy his free time in the camp brothel. Christoph liked the idea and he smuggled a shortwave radio in from the city. Klaus was not thrilled to get help from a known criminal but realized this was the only way he could get news about the war and receive coded messages from the partisans to escape from the camp.

Hitler's army swept through Czechoslovakia, Poland, the Scandinavian countries, Belgium, Netherlands, and Russia, but the Russian front started to block the advancement, and push out the German army from occupied countries. American forces also pushed out the German army from France, Belgium, and the Netherlands. It was March 1944 when Hitler's army lost almost all conquered countries and were pushed back to Germany. The German army torched everything valuable from the occupied countries, killed hundreds of thousands of people from non-German countries, including Jewish, Polish, Russian, Roma people, and Communist sympathizers from Germany.

The American army headed towards Munich, the headquarters of the Nazi party and birthplace of Nazism. At this point a handful of Nazi cadets operated Dachau concentration camp, all the hard-core Nazi military leadership had run away towards the north close to Berlin because of the approaching American army in the south. Klaus realized this was the time to make plans to escape from this horrible place where thousands of people were suffering from malnutrition, disease and extermination by lethal gas. The continuous belching of smoke from burning human corpses in the crematorium filled the air with a stench of death throughout the camp. The emaciated human body barely could keep walking, only protruding eyes emanating a silent message, "I am alive and I exist!"

Klaus developed an escape plan. He would create an electrical short-circuit in the night that would make the camp dark because of power failure. To restore the electricity, it would take a minimum of ten minutes. During this blackout, a selected group of prisoners would pass through a hole in the barbed wire and cross the narrow canal and out of the camp. Partisans would pick them up and arrange their passage through an underground tunnel into the forest.

It was April 4, 1944 midnight. The new moon was barely visible in the sky; the darkness of the night covered the whole camp; only a high beam of light scanned the camp every three minutes, piercing the dark night. This was necessary to prevent air attacks from the American bombing squad. Suddenly, the high beams of light vanished into darkness. Two human bodies covered with black paint came out of Barracks 23. A group of guard dogs came close to these humans in silence, only their fierce glowing eyes seen in the darkness. The dogs tumbled to the ground with a whimper. The men ran towards the fence and cut open a part of the fence and ran through it to the narrow canal. A group of people from Barracks 21 came out in the pitch-black field and ran through the fence. A large commotion broke out among the cadets. They started shooting in the dark as all lights were out. Some cadets grabbed torch lights and could see nothing moving, only darkness of the night prevailed.

The next morning a few Gestapo arrived in the camp. A Gestapo officer ordered a roll call for all barracks. They discovered ten people missing in the lineup, two from barracks 23 and eight from barracks 21. They ordered an extensive search around the camp and nearby forest. The search resulted in the capture of six prisoners. They found Klaus, Edith, Angelika, Sheeler and Christoph in the forest hiding in an underground tunnel. The German intelligence officers knew the existence of tunnels in the forest near Dachau. The communists, built tunnels during the purge, when Hitler became the Chancellor of Germany. The Nazi cadres arrested hundreds of communists. To avoid jail and torture by Nazi, many German communists hid themselves in deep forest around Dachau and other nearby cities by digging underground tunnels.

They searched each prisoner to extract information for who was responsible for this escape attempt. Gestapo repeatedly raped Edith and Angelika. Angelika became mute after the torture and rape. Christoph, the Kapo told the Gestapo officer that Sheeler, the communist and Klaus were the masterminds of this escape attempt. He took part in this scheme so he could extract all information and pass it to the camp commandant in due time. The Gestapo officer Captain Russo ordered Klaus, Sheeler, and Christoph to face a firing squad the next day for committing a crime against the fatherland.

In front of her own eyes Edith experienced the inhuman torture inflicted on her body, mind, and soul; she had to live to suffer the demise of her loving husband Klaus and complete decimation of her daughter Angelika's life. This agonizing, unbearable tormented life took away Edith's everyday strength and hope and she succumbed to typhus, which extinguished her life a few months from the escape attempt. Angelika became an orphan in hell.

A Kapo named Henry Klein was notorious in the camp for his brutality over prisoners, but somehow, he developed a very soft spot for Angelika and encouraged her to draw. He brought a slate and chalk for her to draw pictures. All prisoners under Kapo Klein received very harsh work details, but for Angelika he assigned her to stitch the prisoners' clothes. After work Angelika would receive a little extra spoonful of food or porridge or soup. Many in the barracks hated Angelika. Some tried to take away food from her but Kapo Klein castigated them for their misdeed. One day he called Angelika to follow him towards Barracks 21. Then he showed her an area below a window in the barrack's rear side which was whitewashed with white paint, and said to Angelika, "This is your canvas; you can draw here anything you want. Take this block of charcoal for your drawing." Angelika tried to say something but she could not utter meaningful words. Only a guttural sound came out from her windpipe. An ethereal smile burst open to greet and thank Kapo Klein in silence.

The rumors of German defeat circulated in the camp; SS soldiers forced thousands of prisoners in Dachau camp to move to southernmost Germany by foot to avoid the Allied army. During this strenuous journey hundreds died because of starvation, physical exhaustion, and those who could not keep up with a long march were shot to death by the German army. During the march hundreds tried to flee, but most were shot. Hundreds survived the ordeal and liberated themselves from the death camp as free men.

On that white canvas Angelika drew a mural with black charcoal — a piece of burned human remnant. The mural had a barbed rectangular space adorned with two black butterflies fluttering their wings, some dead butterflies lying on the ground and a small gate wide open. A human corpse lay outside the barbed rectangle. At the bottom of the mural, a small inscription which reads, "Hope."

On April 29, 1945 Dachau concentration camp was liberated by the US Seventh Army. The Army did not encounter any resistance from the German soldiers who surrendered. Hundreds of prisoners came out from their barracks and greeted the American army. Most of the prisoners were malnourished. A sergeant from the US infantry division entered Barracks 21 and found a girl curling her tiny body in a twisted ball. Her body was pale, bones were sticking out, and only skin was holding them together. Her large blue eyes bulged out from the eye sockets as if life hung in a string in silence.

The soldier came close to her and asked, "What is your name?" No answer came from the girl; only a guttural sound came from her mouth. The soldier asked a medic to check her health and gave some canned food to her. She ate food like she had eaten nothing for days. The medic checked her vitals, found she was dehydrated and suffering from complete malnourishment. He gave her salt tablets and water, so she could avoid damaging shock and transported her to hospital.

The American army demolished all the barracks; a soldier who noticed the picture on the wall saved the precious mural of Angelika, and he took a picture of it. Angelika survived the war but she never could talk again. Silence was the sound of the soul where suffering, torture, killing, destruction, and all other inhuman bestiality mankind could impose on other humans lived for eternity, through the expression of nothingness and mute without boundary, form, or color — only the existence!

THE PROMISE

Varanasi — the sacred city where dying will bring Moksha to the dead person. No more birth and rebirth so that attainment of Nirvana is secured for the soul who just left the flesh — only the ultimate freedom—no more bondage, lust, no more day-to-day chores that maintains the life filled with family, children, and the boredom of living life.

Om Puri and his family lived in a spacious home in Varanasi close to the sacred river Ganges. It was a joint family where the Puri clan had shared the home over a century. Before his death Om saw his children, grandchildren and great-grandchildren live in harmony in the house. He died at an early age of eighty-two years. His father and grandfather both lived hundred years before the Lord Yuma came and took them away with him. Om had six children; three older ones were boys and the remaining three were girls. He was happy as God gave him boys and girls so he could enjoy living with many grandchildren.

After Om Puri's death, the oldest son Mahendra along with other siblings converted a part of the house into an Ashram for very sick people who would die soon. The house was over a hundred years old; they divided it into two parts, one side for family members to live and the other side for rooms to rent to guests. They built six small rooms, each about 15' x 11' for guests. The family side had three flats, each with two rooms. They built two latrines for the family members to use and two other latrines for the renters to use in their side of the rectangular home. The century-old temple stayed in its own place. They built a kitchen to serve the guests. The old house went through extensive transformation so that a new Ashram could be built and rented. They incorporated vacant land in the plan so that the Ashram would have enough space to accommodate additional rooms. This business model to rent people who wanted accommodation in Varanasi was in demand and a profitable enterprise. But Mahendra and his siblings wanted to help families who were experiencing financial hardship.

Each guest family paid Rs.2000 for the room and board per month, which was very minimal compared to other homes nearby. This was Mahendra's idea to provide a charitable contribution to various families burdened with ailing and aging members. These benevolent activities made Mahendra a leader in the society. He always mentioned his father was happy in heaven and sending him blessings for this good social deed.

Shiv Prasad Agarwal lived in old Delhi where he had a small grocery store. He and his wife Kamla had one son named Kishan. They struggled all their lives and raised their son to believe in God and follow a path of righteousness. Kishan worked very hard to help his father whenever he had holidays during his studies. He excelled in school and graduated with high honors. Then he finished high school and pursued an engineering degree at Delhi University and graduated with flying colors. After graduation from engineering college a coal company hired him as an operations manager. Within two years he received promotion and moved up because of his work ethic, ability, and operational management expertise. After seven years working with the company he was transferred to the headquarters in New Delhi.

After moving to New Delhi, he built a large home and requested his father to sell his old small brick house in old Delhi and move to a new home. His father kept the old house and rented it, so that some money would come.

Time passed by, Kishan married and had two children. Shiv Prasad and Kamla loved their grandchildren and taught them how to be nice and kind to people and follow the path of righteousness. The grandchildren grew up and moved out to a private boarding school for their studies. Kishan was busy managing the coal company and became the chief executive officer of the company. Shiv Prasad and Kamla felt nobody needed them anymore. They were not happy even though they were affluent, but the beauty of life that they enjoyed before was missing.

Kamla developed high blood pressure and diabetes, which took away her eyesight and within two years she passed away because of cardiac arrest. This sudden departure of Kamla devastated Kishan and Shiv Prasad. Kishan loved his mother and always thought she was a part of Goddess Ma Durga. Shiv Prasad missed his wife and prayed to Lord Shiva that he should grant him the salvation so he could join his wife.

Since Kamla's death ten years went by. Routine medical checks revealed Shiv Prasad had high blood Prostate-specific antigen (PSA). Subsequent extensive clinical tests and digital examination confirmed he had prostate cancer. The oncology specialist recommended surgery and chemotherapy. Kishan placed his father in the best hospital in Delhi and hired the best-known cancer specialist to take care of his father's health.

A couple of months later, the doctor told Kishan his father's cancer has progressed to all his organs and no medication and radiation would stop the disease. He would die within six months. Continuing the chemotherapy will do no good. The doctor said he would prescribe medication to reduce the pain so he would not suffer much.

Kishan recalled thirty years ago his father once told him he wanted to die at Varanasi so he could achieve moksha. On that day he promised his father he would take him to Varanasi so he could die in peace and achieve moksha. After hearing the doctor's final prognosis, he realized the time has arrived to fulfill his dad's wishes.

Kishan made a plan to take his father to Allahabad first, then to Varanasi. The first leg of the journey was to fly from Delhi to Allahabad, stay there few days and rest. He wanted to surprise his dad by taking him on a boat ride to the intersection of the meeting point of three Rivers, known as Triveni Sangam. The three rivers were the Ganges, Yamuna and the Saraswati meeting together in one of the most sacred spots in India for centuries. Hindus believed bathing in this Triveni area would wash away all bad karma and misdeeds and purify their mind and soul. This purification of soul would free them from rebirth.

Shiv Prasad never thought he would bathe in the Triveni Sangam in his lifetime. This transformative experience made him cry with joy even though he was going through severe pain in his ribcage. They rested for three days in Allahabad, then boarded the Poorva Express train to reach Varanasi. After reaching Varanasi railway station they took a taxicab to reach their destination, Shanti Ashram.

Kishan rented a room at Shanti Ashram for a long-term

stay. He took a leave of absence from his chief executive officer position at the coal company so that he could look after his ailing father. They received a small room with two cots made from bamboo. A small wooden "Alna" with four racks to place clothes and a table with two drawers to keep valuables like watch, phone and other important items were also there. The drawers locked with a key. One ceiling fan tried to keep the room cool, as the temperature outside was near 100°F. One side of the Ashram three latrines stood for use by the occupants of the Ashram. They were clean, but the stench of urine mixed with naphthalene balls produced a burning sensation in the nose and eyes. There was also a kitchen to make three meals a day—all vegetarian food; no onion and garlic were allowed.

One month passed by since Kishan and his father arrived in Varanasi Shanti Ashram. One night, Shiv Prasad felt a severe pain in his ribcage, the sternum. Kishan called the doctor to check his father's health. The doctor checked him and an X-ray report showed his bone structures had reached a point where they could break and collapse any time without warning. Also, Shiv Prasad had edema in the heart. Doctors prescribed more painkillers to relieve the pain.

It was evening. The Shiv temple in the Ashram started the "Aarti". The priest lit many lamps to offer light to the Lord Shiva. He held a lighted oil lamp in his right hand and a bell on his left hand. He started to move the lighted lamp in a circular motion while ringing the bell. Both hands were following a circular motion synchronized into a dance, offering prayers to Lord Shiva. Strong fragrance emanated from the lighted incense and chanting slokas created illusionary surroundings in the Temple.

Shiv Prasad was lying on his cot and he felt an acute pain

on his left side of the chest, and developed spasms, gasping for air. Kishan was sitting next to his dad's cot. He tried to help his father to breathe but with a loud hiccup he stopped breathing. Kishan called the hospital for an ambulance, but when an ambulance came to pick up Shiv Prasad he had passed away. It was too late to do anything.

The next morning Kishan with the help of neighbors of the Ashram carried the body in a funeral procession to the cremation ground near Manikarnika ghat. They rested shiv's dead body on a wooden funeral pyre. Kishan lit the fire and poured ghee on the burning sandalwood that engulfed his body in a massive flame. Kishan looked at the fire. His eyes welled up and prayed to Shiva to grant moksha to his father.

When the body was completely cremated, Kishan collected ashes in a clay container and took a dip in the river Ganges and poured his father's ash in the flowing river.

A Baul was singing in a nearby narrow road, the song of salvation where he said,

I am floating on air,
Following the way to reach the end of my journey
Where my freedom awaits,
As my life's light dimmer to a complete darkness.

Moksha came close to me,
Touched my cold body,
Sang the song of death
That led into ultimate ecstasy,
Death could bestow on me.

I leave my chariot
Carried by Jetstream for the last time,

My song on salvation also dies with it!

I became a part of moksha for eternity.
No more pain, pleasure, sadness can touch me,
I am above them;
I embrace death with happiness, serenity
And silence will follow me.

Shanti Ashram is a unique place to live. You can see the new life is born one side of the Ashram; the other side you come across people who are waiting to leave this life where they could meet Nirvana and escape the cycle of birth and rebirth. The children running around the courtyard, some play soccer in a close by field. Young lovers embrace each other under the Saal tree. You can hear the arguments between family members in flats around the Ashram. Cries of newborn babies danced on the breeze and the soft melodies vibrate on the strings of a sitar, and you can see a wandering "Baul" singing the song of solitude and redemption.

Some days one can come across a funeral procession carrying a dead body covered with golden yellow marigold garlands heading towards the ghat. Once the procession reaches the cremation ground, members of the funeral party would place the body on the wooden pyre and light the fire. They feed the rising fire with melted butter and sandalwood chips to minimize the odor of burnt hair and flesh. The chanting of slokas purify the human spirit and carry the human soul to the great abode of the God.

Shanti Ashram and its surrounding is like a miniature world where a group of humans live among nature including trees, animals, ponds, river and go through a cycle of life and death which includes life's passion, sadness, laughter, pathos, and a strong desire to live and exist as best someone can. That cycle of eternity embraces time, space and unknown void as the enchanting black hole that subsume everything mortal and immortal. Could that be the Nirvana? Or could it be an illusion which does not exist?

DOMINIQUE

It was time for me to leave the noisy bar. But there was no place to go. My place, well... It was lonely and filled with silence. I asked the bartender to give me another drink. At least these red drops of merlot would fill my stomach and put me into a world away from problems, sufferings, and frustrations.

I guess I was drunk. My stomach was not yet used to this new habit. It protested every time and brought nausea. Yet, I drank because it was the salvation for my agonizing life.

I was thinking of Dominique, she would be thirty-five today. Ten years ago, I met her at a party. She was a thin, bright eyed woman who listened to everything with a passionate zeal. Her deep meaningful eyes caught me on the spot. I was in love with her. The next thing you know, I married her.

As time passed by our relation started to diverge. My intense love was not enough for her. She was unhappy. Her expectation was too much for me, so I gave up. She complained that I could not satisfy her desire; it always frustrated her about everything. Her physical gratification was so demanding that I started to feel I was a slave at the mercy of her whims. We both became disenchanted about life.

Borderline diabetes had been a part of my life for four years. This condition led to sporadic painful calf muscle spasm in my right foot. I developed peripheral arterial disease (PAD) which impaired the blood flow to the pelvic region and the penile artery that resulted occasional erectile dysfunction. This physical condition along with stress, anxiety, and a sense of hopelessness manifested into a chronic sexual dysfunction. She cursed me, tortured me mentally for my inadequacy. She even took away my manhood by publicizing my sexual inadequacy to my family and friends. One day she ran away from me with a young man who was in his early twenties. That was three years ago. I had not seen her since.

I was thinking about her. Her bright brown eyes, dark eyebrow, sharp pointed nose, thin lips painted with glossy lipstick — all came to my mind as real. I felt a strange excitement in my mind and body. A sudden desire crept along my navel to the groin. I took another glass of Cointreau and swallowed it. A hot, burning sensation ran along my gut. I got up from the stool and started walking like a child who could keep himself erect. My head was light, stomach heavy, but with a sense of erotic high, I kept on walking towards the exit. A cool breeze kissed my whole existence as soon as I stepped outside the bar. I felt rejuvenated and liberated from the stifling stench and damp atmosphere of the bar. I was happy and started to whistle a tune. A woman standing outside the bar came close to me and asked, "Do you need company?"

"Yes," I answered. She held my hand with confidence and wrapped my back with her hand. Her gesture would appear to an observer as if we were old friends. Her touch, embrace and perfume brought in my mind's eye the same picture, same texture of my own Dominique.

We walked hand-in-hand for quite some time and then she guided me into a small hotel. The hotel clerk knew my companion, and he greeted her. He said to her, "How is business?"

"Couldn't be better," she answered with a smile. I signed the register, paid the clerk and smiled at him bashfully like a boy who was caught cheating during an examination. But within a second, my bashful look transformed into a special smile of a proud owner of a beautiful woman. The clerk smiled back and winked at us.

The room was spacious and decorated with modern furniture. A Bible was lying on the table, asking everybody why it had to see various sinful acts of love making, as if it had a voice of its own. It appeared to me that the management of the hotel knowingly placed this holy book in purgatory... If God existed, then someday He would put us into hell.

I paid my woman the money we had negotiated beforehand. She took the money, kissed it with gratification and placed it inside a concealed pouch within her purse. She stroked my hair with tenderness, caressed my chest with a suppleness, and suddenly bit my nipple. I was hurt but I liked the sensation of that painful but tingling feeling. It aroused me. I took off my clothes and sat on the bed. She stood in front of me. With the delicate movement she took off her blouse and folded it on the dresser. In a seductive art of striptease, she peeled off her undergarments which were covering her smooth flesh. She danced in the air to show her beautiful body. It amazed me to find out her inner beauty, which she guarded for her customers. She came very close to me and placed my hand on her huge breasts. I could feel the softness of her flesh; my sensation became acute and receptive. I closed my eyes in anticipation of erotic ecstasy.

I could hear a sweet, melodic resonance in my ear. That resonance vibrated on my lips, chest, belly, and my whole existence. A moist, warm gel probed the middle of my rib cage, and then circled on the surface of the navel. A ticklish sensation ran through my spinal cord. The slimy warm liquid traversed further down, and stopped there, waiting for the final summons. That disruption in the finite world of pleasure was a sign of death. I started to shiver. I wanted to scream, but no sound came out only a whisper, "Dominique" from my windpipe.

A beam of soft light radiated through the silk curtain, as if it awakened me to a rainbow playing hide and seek with the darkness of the room. I tried to recall the incident which had occurred the previous night. I could feel Dominique was with me. It was absurd, as time extended into past, present, and future but that feeling lingers.

I found a scribble on the mirror written with lipstick and it read, "It was wonderful. Love, Dominique." I got up and dressed, rushed down the stairs to the hotel lobby and asked for my Dominique to the same clerk who had attended us last night. He told me he had no idea where she could be found. I went straight to the bar, but she was not there. Nobody would remember seeing her.

THE NIGHT

The sun sets in the western horizon, and sparkles in bright red reflection. The dusk approaches slowly like a dark veil spread out all over the horizon. Night follows with its depth of darkness as time passed by. The city which is filled with noise, smoke and human activities dies down suddenly like an empty space by the touch of an unknown magician. The florescent light glitters on the bosom of darkness like a diamond filled necklace of a prostitute. Sometimes a taxicab passes by in a hurry and its glowing eyes pierce the darkness as a comet. A drunk move slowly in his unbalanced steps and sings a tune in an untuned voice.

Within the hidden stomach of the city of red lights, noise oozes out as slime. The smoke of nicotine, perspiration and other human exudates vaporizes into a horrible stench. A hellish "*gazal*" comes out from the gutter of the whorehouse. Before reaching the last stage of its death under the canopy of the dawn, the night wildly submerge itself into the pleasure of flesh like a bastard indulges himself into the hellish orgasmic ecstasy. Those nocturnal animals lie down their tired body under the cradle of the night. The sleep creeps in their body and their physical consciousness metamorphosed into the unconscious, where every pain or pleasure is dead.

At last, the night gets its freedom!

THE CASTLE

In the middle of the castle yard, there is a cavernous deep well. I look down to see how deep it is, but I could not see the bottom of the well. It must have been at least one hundred feet deep.

Teutonic knights might have thrown some people into it, just to enjoy their victim's agonizing cry as they drop down, their screams echoing through the tunnel that raises the hair on your skin in horror.

I went on top of the lookout tower to see how the city looked below. As I climbed the steps, which were in a perfect spiral, my head felt lightheaded. I sat on the step to take some fresh air. I breathed deeply, but the thick, stagnant air filled my lungs. I closed my eyes and rested awhile. When I reached at the top of the tower, I looked at the brick walls where a little inscription read, "Save me." Some dried blood stain was around this inscription. I wondered who scrolled it, and how long ago. Suddenly, I heard a murmur, "Don't look at me, just move forward and follow me to the corner of the tower." I froze; my heart started to thump; my hair on my skin stood up with an unknown fear. I felt something was behind me. Suddenly I heard a loud scream, "Achtung!"

The alarm clock is ringing loudly; I am in my bed, sweating profusely. I cannot get up to stop the sound of the alarm clock. I am paralyzed. I cannot move; only the alarm lingers on. I am relieved to know that it is a dream, but I swear I heard that whisper, "Save me."

CPSIA information can be obtained
at www.ICGtesting.com
Printed in the USA
BVHW031201140321
602506BV00011B/275

9 781788 307956